80's Baby

The Crack Cocaine Epidemic

A Novel by:

Shawn "Nutt" McDaniel Sr.

Copyright © 2020
Shawn McDaniel Sr.

All rights reserved. No parts of this book may be used or reproduced in any manner whatsoever without written permission, except in the case of brief quotations and reviews. Contact the author.
This is a work of fiction. Names, characters, places and incidents are a product of the author's imagination or used fictitiously and are not to be construed as real. Any resemblance to actual events, places, organizations, or persons living or dead is entirely coincidental.

Acknowledgements

I want to thank GOD for giving me another chance to get it right. Next I want to shout out to everyone that has been helping me. Wifey, my parents, siblings, children and everyone else. Thank you all so much. Especially my business partners and other business establishments such as Exclusive Wear, Crystell Publications, Deaf Boy Records, Special Needs Express, Kite Magazine, Don Diva, Life After Death Publicationz, Straight Stuntin' magazine and Wells Awareness.

Author's Notes

As an author and CEO of NSG PUBLICATIONS I feel I have done a great job building my brand from several different Federal prisons. Now that I've been released, I'm going to push even harder. Life after a decade in U.S.P'S and F.C.I'S was very difficult for me. A lot has changed and people are not the same as I remember. Most of my peers are dead, in prison, or out here hustling backwards. Don't get it twisted, I know a few good men that are handling their business. Big entrepreneurship. Shout out to Congo, Big Tone, Kite Magazine, Don Diva and Katrina Breier, my editor.

Therefore - as an ex con, I can stare any youth in the eyes and tell them that all the money in the world is not worth the risk. I lost everything and my children grew up without me, not to mention one of my closest friends was killed by a Cincinnati police officer.

As a closing statement I would like to say, "COME ON Y'ALL, LET'S FIND A NEW, LEGIT WAY TO GENERATE WEALTH."

Shawn "Nutt" McDaniel Sr.

Prologue

From the entrance of the kitchen, Lil' Mac watched helplessly, as his mother laid sprawled out on the floor getting beat over the head with a tire iron by her boyfriend, Greg. Tiffany's hands reached out for Lil' Mac, with a plea of help in her eyes. Blood was gushing from several different head wounds. She was losing a lot of blood, and slowly fading into unconsciousness.

"Help me," she pleaded, her words barely audible.

"Bitch, shut the fuck up," said Greg, through clenched teeth. "I told yo' ass about trying to hold out on me."

He stopped for a moment, then raised the tire iron high above his head, bringing it down in a crushing blow, that undoubtedly killed Tiffany. As if nothing had just happened, Greg probed Tiffany's pockets, turning up a small baggie of crack. He frantically pat searched himself, until finding a broken car antenna. He packed it, and then struck his lighter at the end of the stem. He sucked hard.... coughing up a crack smog.

Greg, through hazed eyes looked up and saw Mac in the door-way. Fear ran through every vein in his little body. Greg stood awkwardly as Mac bolted for the front door. The terrified child fumbled with the locks, until he finally got it open. Then he ran out into the middle of the street and was nearly hit by a passing car, but Mac kept right on running, crossing the street over to Ms. Patty's house. He pounded on the screen door, until Ms. Patty opened up, "Boy, what is your problem?!" Mac turned, pointing at his house. "My momma! He killed my momma!"

Every night Mac had the same nightmare. And tonight was no exception. He would always wake up at the same part of the dream, when he's yelling "My momma!"

Mac, wasn't the only one being awaken by his past. His cell mate Pleasant El, would also be awaken by Mac's screams. The tossing and turning in the bottom bunk told a story of it's own. Pleasant El, had been understanding about the matter because he knew about the demons most prisoners have deep within. Pleasant El, was an old convict turned Muslim. He'd been in and out of the system his entire life. But this time the judge gave him life due to his extensive criminal history. He'd always try to kick knowledge to the younger brothers doing time in 'Jackson State Penitentiary', often inviting them to Muslim service. Mac, was often invited by Pleasant El, but he'd always decline. Mac figured if all that shit they were kicking was so beneficial, then why were all their asses locked up in here with him? He wasn't trying to hear no black power shit.

But for the most part he and Pleasant El got along. Pleasant El, had never asked Mac what his nightmares were about. But he'd always tell Mac to seek some help once he got out. After serving eight years it was time for Mac to re-enter the world as he knew it.... But Help was the last thing on his mind. Money and Revenge was his top priority.

Chapter One
Ten Years Ago

"Boy, calm down and tell me what's wrong," said Ms. Patty.

"He killed my momma," cried Mac.

"Oh my God," Ms. Patty said as she pulled Mac into the house and closed the door.

Baffled, she escorted Mac over to a large sectional couch and sat him down next to her cat. Ms. Patty immediately picked up the phone and called the police, while peeking through her front blinds across at Tiffany's house. She could see Tiffany's boyfriend Greg open the front door, then step out onto the porch. He appeared to be looking for Mac, as he looked up and down the street. "Mac!" He yelled. Then focused his attention towards Ms. Patty's house.

Ms. Patty pulled a 32. Caliber revolver from her large bra and cocked its hammer. "Come over here if ya' ass want to," she whispered, holding the gun tightly. 911 had her on hold, as they always do. Greg, turned around and went back into the house closing the door behind him.

"Hello, may I help you?" asked the 911 operator.

"It's about damn time. Yes, I want to report a homicide," snapped Ms. Patty- as she gave the address to Mac's house.

"We're sending a unit," said the operator.

Mac, could not stop crying. He had his head in his lap crying his lungs out. Ms. Patty wanted so bad to go over and console him, but she wanted to keep an eye on the house. A few minutes later Greg exited the house carrying a laundry basket full of clothes and a small shoe box under his arm. He rushed towards his battered white Ford Escort, and threw the items into the hatch of its trunk. He raced around to the driver's side door and climbed in through the window. He started the car and backed out of the drive-way, then sped off down the street leaving a thick cloud of exhaust smoke in the middle of the street. Ms. Patty watched as the car back fired and jerked and fade in the distance. She left the blinds rushing over to tend to Ramon- as only Ms. Patty called him. She didn't speak a word. She just wrapped her big warm hands around Mac's tiny frame pulling him close to her. She rocked back and forth while looking up at the ceiling.

Ms. Patty, had a hand in raising Mac. Every day before and after school he would go over to Ms. Patty's to eat breakfast and dinner- she'd even pack him a lunch. Ms. Patty was of no kin to Mac, she was a retired insurance sales rep who just so happen to take a liking to Mac. She was aware of his mother's crack habit which often over shadowed any possibility of food being bought with the two government assistance check's Tiffany received twice a month. Mac, had never met his father. He was killed in a bad drug deal when Tiffany was pregnant with Mac. Tiffany started calling him Mac after his father because Ramon Sr. was a true Mac and a pimp. He had turned Tiffany out to ho'in as soon as she turned sixteen. Now they both were dead.

After more than an hour Ms. Patty saw a lone Detroit police squad car pull up to the curb of Mac's address. Angry, she bolted out front door and yelled at the two Caucasian officers. "Are you serious?" She yelled, meeting the officers in the street. She explained briefly what little she knew as she led them back to her house, where Mac laid on the couch still shell-shocked, and crying his heart out.

One of the officer's kneeled down in front of Mac and tried to get him to talk, 'Hey little fella. Would you mind looking up at me and speaking with myself and my partner'- Mac didn't respond. "What's his name?" asked the officer.

"Ramon, but everyone calls him Mac," advised Ms. Patty.

"Mac, my name is Officer Thomas and this is my partner

Officer Luke. I understand that you have witnessed something quite frightening. But I need for you to try and be a big boy for me and tell me exactly what happened. Can you do that for me?"

Again Mac said nothing. He was no longer sobbing, but tears were still streaming down his yellow face. The officer didn't press the issue, he figured maybe Mac was too traumatized to talk and that he just needed some time. The officer's excused themselves leaving Ms. Patty to attend to Mac, while they crossed the street to Tiffany's house. To their surprise the front door was not locked. They did a knock and announce drawing their pistols before entering the house.

A strong stench filled the air, it was a combination of dirty linen, crack smog, foul body odor, and beer. The two officer's both terrified, inched through the living room looking right to left. The younger of the two nearly shitted himself after stumbling over a half-filled beer can.

Tiffany's feet could be seen from the entrance of the kitchen door. "Over here," said one of the officer's motioning his partner. They holstered their guns and stood motionless staring down at the gruesome scene. Tiffany's head was the size of two pumpkins, literally. Deep wounds continued to gush blood forth. Her entire body was in a pool of blood. The two officer's didn't bother checking for a pulse, from the looks of it they were certain she was dead. They immediately called in their findings, and stayed close to the body until the crime scene unit and the homicide division arrived.

The one story HUD house would soon turn into a circus. The cops had to blocked off the street due to the severity of the crime, also because the channel 4 action news was covering the story live from the scene. After several hours the moment everyone had been waiting for, the body bag came wheeling down the stairs and into the back of a white van. The excitement was over. It had been confirmed that Tiffany was dead. The on-lookers started back for their houses, where they would call around gossiping and trying to see if the camera caught a glimpse of them on the ten o'clock news.

Almost no one was concerned about Mac, with the exception of Ms. Patty. Homicide detective Graves was the lead detective on the case. He had already got a detailed statement from Ms. Patty, but truth be told it wasn't enough to issue a warrant. The only thing Ms. Patty could honestly testify to, was that she saw Greg leaving the house. The actual murder had been witnessed by Mac alone, and detective Graves needed Mac's cooperation if he was going to get his name.

Mac, totally shut down. He wouldn't even look up at the detectives or the social worker who was also there to assist in Mac's grieving. The social worker was a middle aged white woman about 250lbs of fat. She stood impatiently as the detective continued to try and get Mac to talk.

"Listen, maybe we should just transport him over to the group home, and hopefully tomorrow he'll be willing to talk," The social worker offered.

Mac's eye's lifted and focused straight on Ms. Patty as if to say, "Don't let them take me," Ms. Patty dropped a few tears as she understood, but said nothing. There was nothing Ms. Patty could have done to prevent the social worker from taking Mac, because she was of no legal kin to him, and besides he was a star witness to a highly publicized homicide. Detective Graves, motioned one of the officer's to take Mac outside and drive him over to the group home.

From the look in Ms. Patty's eye's Mac knew that'll probably be the last time he saw her. As he exited Ms. Patty's house the news reporter rushed towards Mac hurling question after question. The officer raced Mac over to an awaiting squad car, placed him in the back seat and sped off....

Chapter Two

Everything was happening so fast for lil' Mac. Here it was his mother had just been brutally murdered right before his young eye's, and yet instill he was the one riding in the back of a police car, being whisked away from the scene as if he were a suspect. The officer who was driving Mac didn't show any compassion for the young brother. To him he had pretty much seen it all. His only concern was hurrying up and dropping Mac off because it was close to shift change.

After a ten minute drive of complete silence the squad car had reached its destination. The officer pulled to the curb and quickly exited the car leaving its engine purring. He snatched the back door open and motioned his hand to Mac, as if to say 'hurry'. "Come on kid. I ain't got all day to be fooling with you," The young officer said, as Mac scooted out the back seat. The officer walked Mac up a flight of concrete stairs leading to the entrance of a brown brick building that resembled a nursing home. The sign on the door read 'The Mission'. It was a group home for children who had no legal guardian, and a waiting room for those waiting to be adopted.

The officer walked Mac to the front desk and handed him over to the social worker who was in charge of intake. She had been waiting on Mac to arrive. It was as if this was destined to happen the way folks in there were carrying on. The social worker Ms. Tucker, a young black woman probably in her late twenties came from behind the desk and handed Mac some forms to fill out. He didn't bother taking them, he just stood there with his head down trying to hold back the tears welling up. Ms. Tucker asked Mac a few personal questioned, which went unanswered. He had totally went mute and the frustration could be seen on Ms. Tucker's face. "Just have a damn seat then," she snapped pointing to some dusty blue folding chairs. Mac walked over and had a seat.

Kids could be heard in the distance, sounded like playful laughter. Mac however was in no mood to play. As soon as he took a seat Ms. Tucker came from behind the desk and shouted, "You! Come on and follow me." Mac reluctantly got up and followed the mean bitch. She escorted him through a set of double doors and down a long hall, then got on an elevator. They got off on the third floor. "Come on," she snapped leading Mac into a dorm style open area. Bunk beds filled the walls, tables with board games occupied the floor's center, and three TVs were mounted being watched by a large number of kids varying in age and color.

Ms. Tucker, walked Mac to the counselor's office and handed him over to an older white woman named Ms. Weaver, but all the kids called her 'Big Bird', only behind her back though. She was at least six feet tall, two hundred plus pounds, with some big ass feet. But she was sweet as pie. "What's your name?" she asked kneeling down to Mac's height.

"Oh, he doesn't talk," Advised Ms. Tucker. "But he's all yours. Have fun," she teased leaving the officer.

"Don't mind her, she's an ass," said Ms. Weaver. "I have some questions I need to ask, but of course they can wait until later, maybe tomorrow or whenever you're up to it. I can understand you not wanting to talk right off the back, but you should know lots of kids are just like you when they first arrive. Everyone calls me Ms. Weaver, and I expect you to do the same. I am the counselor in charge of your case load. If there is anything I can help you with don't hesitate to ask. But for now lets' find you a bed out on the floor with the rest of the kids. Come on and follow me please," Ms. Weaver concluded, as she escorted Mac out into the common area.

All eyes were on Mac, all the children ceased their activities to see who the new kid was.

"Bring him over here Ms. Weaver," One little voice said.

"Good, see, you're making friends already. Carlos would you please see to it that Ramon is set up for tonight. He's going through a rough time so keep an eye on him for me."

"No problem Ms. Weaver."

"And Ramon I'll be in first thing in the morning to check on you. If you need anything ask Carlos here. You boys be good, I'll see you guy's tomorrow," Ms. Weaver said leaving Mac and Carlos at their bunk beds.

"What up doe my baby ? My name is Carlos. But everybody calls me 'Los'," Carlos said, extending his hand to give Mac a play. Mac didn't bother shaking hands or giving him dap, he just stood there.

"Alright, I feel you. I'm a grab you some sheets and a blanket so you can make your bed. I know you probably want to chill out."

Mac flopped down on his bunk and put the pillow over his face. He didn't give a fuck about no blanket or sheets- Why was he there? Was the only thing on his mind. Exactly what was he doing there? And who said he had to stay? His little mind was racing for a while. He was soon awakened by his own screams from the haunting nightmare of his mother's murder. He sat up in his bunk and looked around with embarrassment showing in his eyes' because everyone was now staring at him. He was certain that everyone heard him scream.

"Are you alright?" asked Los, as he tossed Mac his sheets and blankets.

Mac didn't respond, he just laid back looking up at the bunk on top of him.

"I got some chips and snacks man if you get hungry," Los offered. He was trying to be nice to Mac because he could remember the day he arrived at The Mission, over two years ago. He was a mess, his mother had just overdosed on heroin. Los had come in from school one day and found his mother collapsed in the bathroom with a needle in her arm. The state made him and his four sisters a ward of the state. They all got adopted by different families, all except Los. No one wanted to adopt him because he wasn't the ideal child, he was too old, and in most families eye's he was already set in his ways. As a result he was stuck sitting in The Mission with the rest of the kids who couldn't find a willing family.

Los, shrug, then sat back in his own bunk which was right next to Mac's. He started talking about how long he'd been at the Mission, how he ended up there, and finding his sisters. "Man, hopefully whatever your situation is, I hope it's not that bad because this ain't it right here. I mean it's alright to an extent, but sometimes I feel like I'm in prison," Los said.

Mac wasn't saying anything, but he felt every word Los spoke. He definitely felt like he was in prison. Even though there were no gates or security guards stopping them from leaving, but where were they going to go if they did leave except to the streets. Just like Los, Mac didn't have any family members who were going to step up and take him in. Even with it being just him, his family had been cut its ties with him due to his crack addict, thieving mother. Tiffany had burned so many bridges over the years. She once stole seven thousand from her dying mother, her and her boyfriend Greg broke into Tiffany's mother's safe leaving nothing behind. Mac, had been cutting up in school and gaining the reputation of a trouble maker, so the family figured that an apple didn't fall far from it's tree. They weren't dealing with Mac on no level, on the holidays it was just him, Tiffany, and some crack heads.

    Tiffany wasn't much of a mother to Mac. In fact, she hated when he called her ma because it made her feel old, and more importantly it made her face the fact that she was indeed his mother and she was neglecting him. The only thing Tiffany cared about was herself and getting high. She was still unarguably the baddest chick in the hood, even being on crack. All the dope boys who didn't stand a chance with Tiffany back when she was on her square and deemed 'The Queen', they were especially happy and loving every moment of Tiffany being on crack. Not only did it give them a sense of retribution, but they also got multiple chances to live out their fantasies with Tiffany, for as little as a dime rock of crack cocaine.

At all hours of the night traffic would be flowing through Tiffany's house. It was nothing for Mac to wake up at three in the morning, and walk into the front room and see his mother on her knee's sucking some nigga's dick. Or sometimes she'd be in the doggy style position with one nigga fucking her from the back, while giving another nigga some head. When Mac would see this Tiffany would continue on as if he weren't standing there. Mac had learned not to let that sort of stuff bother him. Deep down he knew it had to be wrong, but it was happening so often that it couldn't be that bad, so he tried to accept it for what it was.

Greg, Tiffany's boyfriend would be right there front and center, not so much watching the orgies. He was making sure all deals went through him because Tiffany would cuff the crack payments on him in a minute. He had whooped her ass on several occasions for holding out on him. To eliminate all that, he would collect all the dope and the money. In the hood they called that 'Gorilla Pimpin'.

Of all the people in the house coming and going. Mac hated Greg with all his heart. He had watched Greg single handedly destroy his beautiful mother. And at least three times a week he watched Greg beat Tiffany's ass all through the house, and sometimes even outside. One day Mac and a few of his friends were outside in the backyard playing basketball on a homemade crate nailed to a telephone pole, when all of a sudden Tiffany came bursting out the back door running for what seemed like her life. Greg was right on her heels. He finally caught her on the side of the house and he started beating Tiffany relentlessly with man punches. Mac, and his friends watched in disbelief, Mac was not only ashamed but also afraid. He had wanted to help his mother so bad on many occasions, but he was too afraid of Greg- Greg, had put the fear of God in Mac...

Chapter Three

Mac, had drifted off to sleep while listening to Los talk about his problems. Listening to Los had brought back so many memories, the kind that makes you sleepy because that's the only way of not dealing with them. At the crack of dawn as promised Ms. Weaver was there to check on Mac. She didn't have any kids of her own and to her, the kids at the Mission were hers and it was her responsibility to make sure they were well taken care of.

Ms. Weaver shook Mac's legs gently, "Ramon. Ramon' she quietly whispered trying not to startle Mac. His eyes began to open and as he came to he jumped up out of not knowing where he was.

"It's okay Ramon. It's okay.' Ms. Weaver said, gripping Mac tightly in her arms. She held him until he calmed down. She had seen this happen too many times when kids first arrived at the Mission. It would take them some time to get use to the environment there. As Mac's heart rate decreased Ms. Weaver eased her grip. She looked Mac in the eyes. "Are you okay now?"

She asked.

Mac didn't respond. He removed himself from Ms. Weaver and sat on the edge of his bunk with his back to her. He put his face down in his hands while he vaguely listened to Ms. Weaver. "Breakfast is over there on the tables. I'll be sure to have Carlos set you something aside. I brought you a hygiene kit, so after you get yourself together try and get some food in your system. I'll be back to check on you after a while, okay," Ms. Weaver said, rubbing Mac's back.

"Man, I got your breakfast. I'm going leave it over there on your night stand," Los said, as he sat two cheese Danishes and a milk on the night stand between their bunks. "You hear me?"

Mac, didn't budge, he was still leaning over with his face in his lap. He wasn't thinking about eating. How could he with all this drama surrounding his life? Mac was only concerned about what happened to his mother, and what was going to happen to him. He held out hope that maybe Ms. Patty would come get him, but he could still see that look in her eyes as he left the house. He could sense that was the last time they'd ever see each other again.

Mac really had love for Ms. Patty. She took good care of him, practically raised him for that matter. When they were alone he'd call her Momma Patty. In many sense she was his mother. She was present for the first day of school. It was her that picked him up whenever he got kicked out of school. And it was her who would take Mac to the doctor, get school shot's, all the while pretending to be Tiffany. But those days were over, she could no longer save Mac from what was ordained to happen. Ms. Patty would make the ideal adoption parent for Mac. But only one thing, Ms. Patty was dying from cancer. She needed what time she had left to herself. She had spent her entire life helping others. Now it was her time to relax, and that was the look Mac had saw in her eyes...

"Anyway, what's your name my baby?" Asked Carlos, as he made his bed, tucking his sheets military style.

"You know you should really start talking because you don't want these clowns around here thinking you're soft. I ain't about to watch nothing happen to you, but I'm just saying, you know?" Los said, as he finished his bed. He continued talking to the air as he groomed his hair, brushing it with one hand and patting it with his free hand while looking in the mirror. Los, was a pretty boy type. He stood about five-eight, light brown skin, green eyes, and deep brush waves. He and Mac could pass for brothers, except Mac had hazel brown eyes, and straight sandy brown hair. They stood almost shoulder to shoulder and weighed about the same.

"Los, yo' slow ass still not ready?" Asked the voice of a young lady. Her voice was filled with attitude and swagger.

It was the most beautiful thing Mac had heard since the

murder of Tiffany. Mac's head rose to see who was talking. The young lady standing before him was drop dead gorgeous. She stood about five-three, thick to death. She was only twelve years old, but she was built like a grown ass woman. Her skin tight jeans and halter top hugged every curve of her body. Her shoulder length silk black hair complimented her soft golden-brown skin. She turned and faced Mac with those big beautiful eyes and looked him up and down. "What you looking at?" she asked.

Mac, couldn't find the words- He just continued to take in the girl's beauty. "Leave him alone Ebony," Los said as he grabbed his coat and back pack.

"Don't' mind her man. Look, I gotta' go to school, so I'm a check you out when I get back, a'ight," Los said.

"Come on," he said, as he grabbed Ebony by the shoulder.

"If they bring one mo' yellow nigga up in here. I swear I'm a scream. You niggas think y'all cute," Ebony said, as her and Los walked out of the dorm.

That was pretty much the scene, all the kids were heading in different directions on their way to school, some skipping school altogether heading for the arcade, other's to their old stomping grounds. As long as you were in before curfew, which was eight o'clock, the administration at the Mission didn't give the kids too much hassle. The only time a counselor or case manager would intervene was when the school's truancy officer would call, but they'd have to miss over thirty days for them to get involved.

For Mac, today was a big day and yet he didn't even know it. His entire day had already been mapped out by Ms. Weaver. At the Mission there was no idol time during business hours because that was the time the big wigs would drop in unannounced. Things had to be in order because they were the ones who determined how much government funding the Mission received, so if they were to see money being wasted they'd cut out that section of the budget at their earliest convenience. And that may very well be someone's job!

Ms. Weaver was a busy-bee. She orchestrated and delegated the entire show. She had been at the Mission since its opening back in the early 60's, yet she was still involved in its daily operations and was as hands on with the kids as any other employee. She handed Mac an all-white box which was made of cardboard. Mac was all too familiar with that box, as he received one for Christmas for the past eleven years of his life. It was the hood famous 'Good Fellow Box'- Every poor kid knew what a good fellow box was. If you ain't never had one, then you weren't poor growing up. Inside was your standard Wrangler straight leg jeans, knitted sweater, socks, drawers, scarf, candy, and miscellaneous school supplies- (i.e. a kid's worst nightmare on Christmas).

"Ramon, I need for you to get dressed quickly because someone is here to see you," Ms. Weaver said, looking at her watch, as she left Mac's bedside.

Mac, grabbed the white box and headed towards the bathroom. He locked the bathroom door once inside because he had heard the stories about being molested in places like the Mission, and it always seemed to take place in the bathroom.

Mac wanted to take a shower because his little arm pits had started to hum. Ms. Patty wouldn't have that, she taught Mac to always stay on top of his hygiene, even if his clothes weren't the best as long as they were clean was all that mattered. After looking at the shower floor, and its walls Mac declined on the idea. There was no way he was about to step barefoot in that shower. It was just plain filthy, so he settled for a bird bath.

After Mac finished grooming himself and tucking his Wranglers behind the tongue of his Air Jordan's, he emerged from the bathroom looking like new money. Mac had that one type of swag, where damn near anything looked good on him. A person was going to look at him first, and then maybe his clothes.

"I see we have another pretty boy on our hands. You and Carlos should get along just fine," Ms. Weaver said, examining Mac from head to toe.

'You look nice. Remind me later to give you a voucher to go

down to the Salvation Army so you can get some more clothes. But right now you have someone here to see you. He's waiting for you in my office," she said pointing towards an open door.

"Close the door, son." It was detective Graves, the lead detective assigned to Tiffany's murder. Mac shut the door behind him, but dropped his head as soon as it shut.

"Have a seat," offered Detective Graves. Mac didn't budge. He was hoping that whatever it was this man wanted wouldn't take long. He knew whatever it was, it had nothing to do with Mac leaving with a family member.

"Okay, well stand. Son, look at me." Mac slowly looked up at the detective. He was an older gentleman. Late fifties, big gut, and going bald. He wore thick Mafia style plastic glasses and had a serious, yet subtle persona about him. "Do you know why I am here?" He asked, looking down at Mac.

Mac shook his head no.

"The man who did this to your mother is out there on the loose. I need your help in order for me to catch him, so he can't do this to anyone else. You do want him to be punished for this, right?"

Mac again didn't speak a word. He only shrugged his shoulders, as if to say 'I don't know.' "Well son, unless you help me the man that did this to your beautiful mother will remain a free man. Did your mother's boyfriend Greg do this?"

Mac didn't answer. At the sound of Greg's name Mac dropped his head again.

"It's okay, he won't be able to hurt you or anyone else. I promise! Was it Greg that killed your mother Ramon?"

"I didn't see nothing. I don't know," Mac said, finally breaking his silence. But his eyes were still on the floor.

"Son, don't do this," said detective Graves, he knew Mac was lying, he'd seen it a thousand times. Kids would often lie to cover for someone out of either love or fear. Detective Graves now had to figure out which one it was in Mac's case if he were to try and play on that.

"Did Greg ever beat your mother in front of you?"

Mac didn't bother answering.

"How about you, did Greg ever beat you for any reason?"- No answer. "Do you love Greg?"

Again no answer. All the questions detective Grave threw out there went unanswered. It wasn't so much that Mac was afraid of Greg to the point where he wouldn't help the police catch him, nor was it that he loved Greg. It was the total opposite, he hated Greg with as much hate as a person could possibly hate one human being, that's how much he hated Greg's ass.

Mac had made his mind up that he would not help the police. He didn't care how long it took, Mac wanted to be the one to catch Greg and kill him. It was beyond personal. Even with Greg killing his mother, before then Mac would sit in his room and fantasize about one day being old enough to kill Greg's ass. There was no way he was going to let the funky ass Detroit Police department get in his way. 'One Day' Mac told himself.

Detective Graves saw that he had hit a brick wall. Mac had shut down again, and he was only beating a dead horse. He decided to wrap the interview up, but knew he'd soon find himself back at the Mission because it had become an overnight highly publicized case. Folks on the radio were calling in talking about it. The news had shown the story on every channel. They went so far as to set up a donation account for burial purposes, and even did a memorial with lit candles and teddy bears on the porch of the house. All the attention the case was receiving no one thought to mention Mac's situation, other than that he was supposedly in the house at the time of the murder. No adoption talk or any family members stepping forward. Just solve the case so people could stop talking about it.

Mac would have several more interviews with mental health personnel at the Mission and other grievance counselor's. Each jugging at what happened in that house. And each time Mac would shut down on them. The interviews took up most of the day lasting through lunch and ending conveniently at three o'clock, which was punch out time for the low-budget doctors. Ms. Weaver was still on deck though. She was always the first one in and the last one out. She would have it no other way. She was concerned with what had taken place as well, but she wasn't the type to impose, especially when she could clearly see that an individual didn't want to discuss their issues. To her, it was about respect. She could see that the day had taken a toll on Mac. So all her questions and paper work would have to wait.

"Ramon, I will give you the voucher tomorrow for the Salvation army. Just try and relax for the rest of the day, and I'll see you first thing in the morning," Ms. Weaver said.

By this time all the kids were coming in from school or from ditching school. Mac was sitting at one of the table's watching TV when he saw his house flash across the screen. They were still conducting the memorial service, people could be seen placing single rose's on the porch and lighting candles. Some were just on-lookers standing by with tears in their eyes. Mac tried his very best to scan the crowd looking for an aunt, uncle, cousin, anybody for that matter who he may have known. No one.... The slight hope of someone coming to save him from this evil nightmare faded as the news switched to the weather.

Los had stepped in from school. He was obviously rushing, as he kicked off his shoes and stripped down to his boxer's. He fumbled through a large wall locker and pulled a pair of mesh gym shorts out and a Joe Dumar's Piston's jersey immediately putting the items on. He sat on the edge of the bed, while he laced his basketball shoe's up. He just so happen to look up and saw Mac sitting in front of the TV with his back to him.

"Aye, what up my baby? I'm about to go to the center and dog these niggas on the court. You can come down there with me if you want too," Los offered.

Mac heard Los but didn't respond.

"Everybody's gone be down there, it's the hang out after school."

Mac thought about Ebony, that young fine thang from this morning. 'Maybe she'll be down there too' He turned around in his chair looking at Los. "Do it be girls down there too?" he asked.

"Yep. Even the one you kept looking at this morning," Los teased.

"Man, I wasn't looking at shorty,"

Los laughed, "It's all good man, everybody has a crush on Ebony. Everybody except me because I been knowing her too long. We like brother and sister."

"I don't want to go down there wearing these," Mac said, pointing down at his wrangler jeans.

"Yeah," Los said, balling his face up in agreement.

'Here, put this on,' he said, tossing Mac a brand new Nike track suit.

"Man, I can't take this from you."

"Don't trip man, I'll get another one. Just hurry up so we can get on the court."

Mac quickly changed clothes after ripping the price tags off the track suit. It was obviously brand new, and by looking at the price on the tag made Mac wonder for a second how Los could afford it, it had to be hot Mac thought.

"What did you say your name was?" Los asked Mac, as they entered the elevator.

"Mac."

"Mac? Like a pimp, player type Mac?"

"Yeah, I guess something like that."

"Where you from?"

"Eureka and 7mile."

"Eastside, huh?"

"What about you?"

"I'm international," Los joked. 'Naw, I'm playing. I just always wanted to say that. I'm from the Westside, Fenkell."

The elevator stopped on the ground floor. Los and Mac stepped off, then blended in with the crowd of teenagers.

"Hey Los," one young lady called out.

"Bitch, don't be speaking to my man," Another girl joked with her friend. 'Hey baby, you ready?" she asked Los.

"Ready for what?" Los asked.

"For some of this pussy.... she whispered in his ear, then stuck her warm, wet tongue inside his ear.

"We'll see," Los said.

"Los..." More girl's called out as they walked into the gym. A few girls were checking Mac out, but right now he was looking more like Los's side kick or stick man. Los had all the girl's wanting him for some reason.

They walked over to the bleachers where Ebony and a few others were seated. Ebony rolled her eyes at Mac as soon as they pulled up, then looked him up and down.

"Who is this?" asked ET.

"Everybody, this is Mac. Mac, this is Ebony, ET, and the groupies," Los said, pointing to the assorted female's sitting in the next row, above them.

"Oh yeah? Fuck you too nigga," One of the hood rat's shot back at Los.

"You wish," Los said.

"Why you bring him over here, we don't know his ass?" Asked Ebony. She had a way of trying to make people feel uncomfortable when she first meet them. It was her defense or should I say front because the girl was actually a sweet heart once she warmed up to you.

"Don't start Ebony. He's with me so y'all already know he's official. Gone head bruh, have a seat Mac, unless you trying to get out here on this court. Can you ball?"

"I'm straight."

"Alright. Well, maybe next time. I'm a be out here schooling these boys, holla if you need me. Here, hold this," Los said as he handed Ebony a large bank roll of money, a pager, and two gold rope chains.

Mac could tell right off the bat who the leader was. He didn't know what Los was doing, although he had an idea. Whatever it was Mac wanted in. He liked the attention all the girls were showing Los. Los's whole demeanor, and how people were listening to him was something new to Mac. He had never met a young boss before.

Mac sat beside Ebony trying his best not to look nervous. His heart was pounding a mile per second, and his throat had all of a sudden gotten dry. He had started praying that Ebony would not say anything to him so he wouldn't have to respond. He was just too nervous to carry a conversation with her. Mac pretended to be interested in the basketball game, not breaking his stare for one second. He could still see Ebony's thick brown thigh from the corner of his eye. 'Oh my god, she smells so good,' Mac thought.

"I just want you to know that you ain't cute," Ebony said, sucking her teeth at Mac.

"Didn't Los tell you to leave him alone?" ET intervened.

"Los don't run me. I'm a grown ass woman. He might run yo' ass but not mines."

"Don't have me call him over here," ET said.

"Don't listen to her she's crazy."

ET was part of the crew, one third of it. It was him, Ebony and Los. They did everything together. If you saw one you pretty much seen all three. It had been that way for the past two years. ET was kind of slow, he had a learning disability so Los looked after him. ET stood about six feet even, about 185 pounds of muscle, and ugly as they come. He was midnight black, with short nappy hair and yellow eyes. ET had a menacing aura about him, and lived up to it every chance he got. He was only twelve but he was built like a grown man. The kids at school and at the Mission didn't dare fuck with him or Los. Shit, you had some grown men who didn't want to see ET with the hands.

Mac continued to watch the game while feeling out of place. As soon as the gym closed everybody went across the street to the Deli, where Los treated them all to burgers and fries. Mac could tell that he wanted to hang with them every day if he had to stay at the Mission. But he still held out hope that someone would come for him...

Chapter Four

Two months had passed and that hope Mac had been holding on to had dwindled. He, just like Ebony, ET, and Los accepted the fact that he would remain at the Mission. The prospect of him being adopted seemed slim to none because of his age. Almost everyone who was looking to adopt a child wanted a new born so they could raise it as one of their own. No one wanted some bad ass child. And that was the perception of kids Mac's age. Ms. Weaver would have adopted all of them, but it wasn't possible in all reality. So, she just made sure that whenever she was at the Mission the kids had the majority of her day. She'd help them with their homework, play board games with them, just about everything a normal parent would do with their kids.

Ms. Weaver enrolled Mac into Miller Middle school. He and Los were in all the same classes, so he would walk to and from school with Los, Ebony, and ET. Their school was about ten blocks over from the Mission, every morning they'd have to walk through the King Holmes projects to get to their school. The King Holmes was a rough little section of the projects, which separated Miller middle school and King high school. When Los and ET first started going to Miller they had several run ins with the kids of the King Holmes projects, and even some grown men. They didn't want Los and ET walking through their shit because they weren't from around there, and also because they were moving drugs out of the projects. Los and ET were nobody's punk though they stood their ground and fought every day until finally one of the older dudes who were running the Holmes told his little niggas to fall back on fucking with Los and ET.

    The man's name was Brick, he was second in command to a nigga by the name of Murder, or Murda' as he pronounced it. Brick like the way Los and ET stood on what they believed in. Most niggas would turn around and run, then start taking the long way to school, having to walk all the way around the King Holmes projects just to get to school. It was a difference of about a mile.

    Brick also saw potential in Los more so than ET. Brick quizzed them on where they were from and if they had ever hustled. Los having sold crack before was up on game how to cook the shit, bag it, and set up shop. He even had a little stash saved up from his days of selling in his old neighborhood. Brick wanted Los to work for him, but over in his own hood. He would front Los the exact same amount of coke that he bought, so if Los bought an eight ball, Brick would front him an eight ball on consignment.

Every Friday after school Los would meet up with Brick and cop his drugs, then head over to his hood by bus to sell it. School was a joke to Los. The only reason he even bothered to show up was because he knew the game. The name of the game was attendance. As long as he showed up for school and went to class the truancy officer couldn't recommend a placement in a juvenile center. It didn't matter that he was receiving all F's on his report card, the court couldn't lock him up for receiving bad grades. That was the game and Los had given the game to ET, Ebony, and Mac. He made sure they all went to school and class, so that they wouldn't' risk the chance of being split up. For them school was just a fashion show, and they were best dress thanks to Los's crack selling.

Friday's couldn't come soon enough. As soon as that three o'clock bell rung, it was show time. Los would go straight to the King projects and cop his shit from Brick, then jump on the public bus and head over to Fenkell. Mac had been on Los ass about him taking him with them this week so he could start making some money. Los really didn't mind Mac coming along, but it was a few niggas on his block with bad attitudes and itchy trigger fingers. Violence was nothing to him. Plus everyone in his hood respect his gangsta'. He just didn't feel like hearing their mouth about him bringing new ma'fuckas to the hood.

"Fuck them ho' ass niggas. If one of them lames got a problem with what we doing, I'll knock they bitch ass out," ET said.

ET rarely said anything. He just sat back and let Los run the show. For them to be so young they had shit in order. They weren't on no little boy shit, most of the kids their age would be somewhere throwing rocks at cars or breaking into houses. It was all business, guess it had to do with all the hardship they had been through. They knew the value of a dollar. For Los it was all about finding his sisters and being a family again. He was putting money away every time he flipped a sack with hopes of one day being granted custody of his sisters. That would be at least seven years from now though.

"Alright listen, when we get over there if anybody ask you where you're from. Just tell 'em your my cousin and you just moved here from Indiana," Los said, going against his first mind. He wanted to see Mac make some paper, he just didn't want it to be at the expense of him making his.

Ebony, would always try to tag along, but Los wasn't having it. He knew that every nigga on the block would only be trying to fuck her young ass. It would be more of a problem because he'd definitely have to put hands on one of them niggas, well ET anyway. Los would walk Ebony back to the Mission, give her some money and then cut out. Curfew on the weekend was ten o'clock but the counselors weren't really tripping. 'Just be in before eleven,' they'd say. That gave Los and them about seven hours to catch the bus, sell their shit, and be they ass inside the Mission by eleven.

"Remember what I said. You my cousin and you're from Indiana," Los said, talking through his teeth as him, ET, and Mac walked up on the block.

They had really gone unnoticed until they made it halfway down the block where most of the activity was taken place. Niggas were playing basketball on a roll out, you had about twenty niggas on the sidewalk shooting dice, people were pulling up in cars back to back as runners served them. Everything was centered around 'The Porch'. The Porch was a vacant house that niggas basically took over. It had been spray painted, all the siding had been pulled off and sold as scrap. Niggas purposely damaged the house so no one would want to rent it. The owner just took it as a lost. That house had a new owner, all the niggas on the block. They called the house simply 'The Porch'.

You could buy almost anything from the porch, weed crack, pills, you name it. You could even buy some pussy on the porch. The inside of the house was a stash spot for nigga's guns, drugs, and chill spot. You had old man Butch, the mechanic out there fixing cars in the drive-way. Lil' Rob was the barber and Will was the DJ selling mixtapes, CD's and bootleg movies. Everybody had a hustle going. 'The Porch' was also street court. If there was a dispute, before it came to violence niggas would say "take it to the porch..." They had a panel of judges and everything, making rulings and shit. It was an all-out comedy show. Niggas making money and clowning while doing so.

"Los is in the ma'fuckin' house," Diamond announced. Diamond was the self-appointed mayor of the porch and critically acclaimed damned fool. 'Who the fuck is this nigga?" Diamond asked.

"Yo' nosy ass always asking questions. Who is that chicken head bitch you got on yo' lap nigga?" Los shot back.

"Who the hell yo' lil mannish ass calling a bitch?"

"You bitch!" ET said.

"Y'all chill out. Now Los you know the porch rules man. You can't be bringing no outsiders to the porch," Diamond said.

"Well, he ain't no outsider. This my cousin Mac. He just moved up here from Indiana."

"They do kinda' look alike," Neisha said.

Neisha was a bull dagger. Bitch looked like a man, she stood about five eleven and weighed close to two hundred pounds. Niggas gave her the upmost respect because she was a rider and plus she kept some bad young bitches on the porch. Neisha sold all the pills on the porch too.

"Well a'ight, I guess the lil' nigga cool then. But Los yo' ass need to start coming around here with a little more respect," Diamond said.

"Yeah, whatever," Los said, brushing past Diamond as he walked into the house. Diamond was really salty at Los because he wasn't working for him like most of the young boys on the block. On top of that Los was bringing his own work to the porch. That shit didn't sit too well with Diamond, especially coming from such a young nigga. But the constitution of the porch stated that anyone who was born and raised on the block had just as much right to the porch as the next man. There was nothing Diamond could do besides let Los do him.

Los and ET rushed towards the kitchen where they grabbed a pot and the Pyrex mixing jar. They were in a rush to cook up them two ounces of cocaine that Los just got from Brick. They weren't trying to miss the rush. Every Friday about five o'clock the rush began, that's when all the white crack heads would flood the block spending no less than a hundred dollars. Friday was check day.

Mac stood to the side as he watched Los and ET go to work. Los dumped both ounces of coke into the Pyrex jar, then measured about a half ounce of baking soda by eye. Seconds later he tossed it on top of the coke. Then he took a spoon and mixed the two together the best he could, while he waited for the pot of water to start boiling. As soon as the water began to bubble, Los set the Pyrex jar down inside the pot and waited about two minutes. He then lifted the jar and swirled it in a circular motion making sure the baking soda was cooking into the coke. Once the coke turned into complete oil base, Los rushed the Pyrex over to the sink, where ET had placed some ice cubes. Los carefully put the jar over the ice and watched the oil turn into a rock hard cookie like form.

Los dumped the block of crack onto a napkin and blotted it dry, then took out a razor blade and began cutting up ten dollar rocks. They didn't bother bagging up the crack, they just grabbed a box of sandwich bags and split up the rocks, evenly between Los and ET.

"So, what y'all want me to do?" Mac asked, staring at Los. None of this was foreign to him, he had watched the hustlers from his neighborhood fuck his mother, cook coke into crack and sell it out of their house his entire life.

"We could use some help," ET said, looking at Los. Los thought for a moment, 'Yeah because niggas gon' be everywhere.' He thought. "A'ight listen, this what we gon' do. We gon' spread out. I'm a take the front. ET you take the end because I want Mac in the middle. Mac all you gotta' do is, when a car pull up, ask 'em what they spending. Once they give you the money you give them they shit. Each one of these is ten dollars. You got it?" Asked Los.

"Yeah."

"A'ight then, let's get out there," Los said, as he handed Mac a sandwich bag full of rocks.

They all filed out the house Los leading the way. "Aww shit y'all. Here come Los and the Gambino family," Diamond joked.

Los was all business, he walked over to his post near the curb, then pointed to where he wanted Mac to stand.

"That's right baby, run yo' shit. Get yo' money Boo," Neisha teased.

The traffic began flowing. Cars were pulling up in pairs and bunches, the rush was on. The cars that got passed Los while he was serving another, it was Mac's job to serve, and if Mac was busy then it fell on ET to serve 'em. The other niggas on the porch were running all over Mac bogarting their way to cars. Maybe a hundred cars had come through and Mac hadn't sold one rock. Diamond was sitting on the porch taking all this in and loving every moment of it.

"A young'in come here." Diamond hollered. Mac was about to go and see what Diamond wanted, but Los spotted the situation. He waved his hand at Diamond as to say 'fuck that nigga. We on the grind'. Mac didn't want to fall out with Los so he kept to his post. It took him a while to get the hang of how niggas were getting their shit off. Niggas weren't taking turns, this wasn't no grocery store line. This was the jungle! You had to get yours or go hungry.

There was no way Mac was going to miss the rush and have to tell Los and ET that he didn't sell one rock. He knew the probability of them letting him come along next time was slim to none. Mac was in no way a punk, he put it in his mind that the next car that made it to him was his. A few seconds later a silver colored Astro mini van pulled up to Mac's post. One of the other young runners sprinted past Mac in attempt to catch the sell. Mac was on the boy's heels. Before the boy could stop Mac hit him with a football style block, sending the boy to the pavement. 'What you need?' Mac asked, the driver leaning inside the driver side window as he seen Los and ET do. The driver handed Mac two hundred dollar bills. Mac then reached down inside his boxer briefs and served the older white gentlemen twenty rocks.

By this time the young boy Mac had knocked the wind out of was on his feet. He was much bigger than Mac and about three years older. His street name was Vito. Without warning Vito charged Mac from behind. He picked Mac up by his legs and slammed him down on the curb. Then he tried to climb on top of Mac. But it was to late, Mac had managed to roll onto his back and he was kicking like a mule. He kicked Vito in the rib cage sending him backwards. That gave Mac enough time to scramble to his feet. The two squared off toe to toe and just as Vito was about to charge

Mac again. Neisha stepped between them. And thank god she did because Vito was about to tear off into Mac's ass. But that's what was going to have to happen because Mac wasn't backing down.

"Take it to the Porch," Neisha said, pointing towards the steps.

Mac and Vito both walked towards the porch mean mugging each other. It was time for court and sanction, which was a fine jar. Whoever is found guilty has to pay a fee. The money inside the fine jar went towards repairs to the porch whenever the police raided and tore shit up. Also, the money was used for bail money and lawyer fees for niggas on the block.

"All rise! Porch is now in session," Diamond said. 'You two niggas need to have a seat'. Neisha said, pointing toward two lawn chairs.

While on trial at the porch you had the right to call any witnesses or present any evidence you wished to support your defense. Mac wasn't interested in none of that shit, to him all this porch shit was a fuckin joke. Vito, though straight snitched in Mac's opinion. "I know y'all seen that nigga hit me from behind," Vito explained his case.

"Yeah, and I also been watching you niggas take advantage of the young'in. None of you ma'fuckas was gon' let shorty hit a lick," Neisha said, taking up for Mac.

"That nigga ain't even from the hood though," Vito said, looking for Diamond to take his side, because he was one of Diamond's workers.

"Vito, you know ain't no rules when you out here serving. Dog was just getting in where he fit in. Niggas be pushing and shoving for sales all day, don't take it personal. And you my man, if you got a problem with somebody over here, we take it to the porch understand?" Diamond said, really not siding with neither side.

"So what you want to do with them?" Diamond asked Neisha.

"I think they both equally guilty, so they can both pay the fine or make an agreement to chill the fuck out," Neisha said.

"What y'all gon' do. Is we all straight?' Diamond asked, looking at Mac and Vito.

"We straight," Vito said, not wanting to pay the fine.

"Yeah, we straight," Mac said.

"A'ight then. Porch is out, you two niggas are free to go," Diamond said, slamming an old wooden hammer down on a yellow page phone book.

"What them niggas talking about?" Los asked, as Mac returned to his post.

"Some bull shit, I'm good."

"They bet not be on shit, because we ain't ducking no rec," ET said. He had already beat almost every nigga ass on the block, including Diamond.

"Fuck them, let's finish gettin' this money," Los said.

For the rest of the day Mac didn't have no problems getting his shit off, he had earned that hood respect every other nigga had to earn. It was like that in every hood. Once niggas knew you weren't going for nothing you got that certain level of respect and had the right to be out on the block. A weak ma'fucka ain't got shit coming...

Chapter Five

Now days, Friday couldn't come fast enough for Mac, which was all he had to look forward to. The hustling and all the fun shit the block provided filled that void in Mac's life. Going to the block every Friday and Saturday with Los and ET had become a ritual. Plus, Mac had started seeing a little money, he had made it to a half ounce of crack in the short time he'd been hustling. With Los it was all love, he wasn't taxing Mac on his shit. Every Friday after school they'd put their money together and Los would go cop from Brick. For Los he just wanted to see his team winning and to shit on Diamond bitch ass while doing it.

Mac had been trying to talk Los and ET into leaving school and the mission altogether. He couldn't understand Los reason for wanting to stay when they were making enough money to rent a house and take care of everything themselves. The money was going to Mac's head, he was thinking about running away from the Mission and try to get somebody from the block to help him get his own spot, if not let him crash at theirs. Mac didn't let Los know about his ideas because he didn't want Los to cut him off before he had the chance to set everything up. And to some extent, Mac felt like he owed Los for putting him in the position to rent his own spot.

Every chance Diamond got he was in Mac's ear about how he should start working for him, and that Los was holding him back. Mac wasn't buying into the notion that Los was holding him back, but he was ready to expand. He just couldn't stay at the Mission knowing that it was his home and knowing that absolutely no one was coming to save him from this nightmare. Mac began to consider Diamond's proposal, but it would be on one condition, that Diamond would help him find a place to live.

"I got you young'in," Diamond told Mac in one of their secret meetings in the kitchen at the house. "A'ight give me until Monday and I'll have things in line," said Mac, nervously agreeing to cross Los and ET out. Mac tried to justify things to himself, telling himself, that it wasn't like he was stealing from them or taking food out of their mouths. But he was missing the point, Los was only looking out for him, he was trying to keep the wolves off Mac. Niggas just like Diamond. Niggas who only wanted to use young niggas and leave them for dead when shit hit the fan. It was about Loyalty, nothing else. A lesson Mac had yet to learn.

Mac played everything smoothly, going to school as usual with Los and ET. Hitting the mall up on Sunday to cop some new gear for the following week, and playing B-ball down in the gym. They had a system of shit they did each day and Los made sure they kept to it so they wouldn't slip off their square. Mac had packed his clothes inside a green army fatigue duffle bag Sunday night, while Los was in the shower. The plan was once everyone went to sleep, which was generally around eleven, Mac would sneak out through the fire escape. By the Mission being a foster care there were no locks on the windows preventing someone from climbing out, nor did they have a security guard at the front desk. So, if a child was to go missing the only legal thing the counselors could do was notify to the police, and that was twenty-four hours later.

Mac had waited until Los closed his eyes and began snoring, then crept out of bed. He slid on his shoes, then got up and walked into the bathroom. He walked over to a linen closet located inside the shower room, reached inside and pulled out the duffle bag he had placed in there earlier. Mac quickly dressed leaving his pjs behind, then climbed out the window onto the fire escape facing the alley. He shut the window behind him, then scanned the alley for any traffic. 'Not a soul in sight,' Mac thought as he climbed down the fire escape. Then he had to hang drop the rest of the way because the ladder didn't reach the ground. Mac ran full speed down the alley, then stopped at the end and peeked around the corner. The side street was deserted, so Mac shot out the alley and sprinted up the street. He was told to walk two blocks over to the BP gas station and call Diamond, then wait for him.

Mac hid behind the gas station and waited until Diamond showed up. After what seemed like forever Diamond's navy blue Caprice Classic pulled into the gas station with the sound system pounding. Mac came racing from behind the gas station flagging Diamond to a stop. He tried to get in the passenger seat, but when he opened the door a young lady already had it occupied. "Nigga' get yo' ass in the back," Diamond said, yelling over the music.

"So you ready to get this money lil' nigga?" Asked Diamond, as he pulled out of the gas station.

"Where you got me staying at?"

"I told yo little ass I got you, didn't I?"

"This lil nigga be trippin'. You ever had some pussy lil nigga?" Diamond asked, looking in the rear view.

"Yup."

"Stop fuckin' lying," Laughed Diamond. 'You hear this lil' lying ass ma'fucka?" He asked the girl he had riding shotgun. She nodded her head laughing, her eyes were almost shut. She was obviously high, as was Diamond.

"I'm not lying nigga," Mac said. He was trying to sound

serious because he was. He had got some pussy a few times. Greg sick ass would make other crack head bitches suck Mac's little dick and give him some pussy. He was too young to bust a nut, but his little dick still got rock hard.

"Nigga.... I said you lying," Diamond teased.

Already Mac could see what type of nigga Diamond was going to be. He was on some fake boss shit, especially when he was around females. That's when he would cut up the most letting it be known that he was the boss calling the shots.

They pulled up to a run down two-family flat, two streets over from the Porch. Mac was looking at the house hoping that this wasn't the place he'd be living in. That hope went right out the window when Diamond killed the engine and said, "Come on and bring your shit ...

"Man." said Mac, reluctantly as he grabbed his bag, then climbed out of the backseat. Diamond led the way up to the front steps of the shack. Crack heads decorated the exterior of the house all of them putting in their bid for some crack "when you gon' let me clean this spot up for a lil something?" One of them asked.

"Shit its cool. We like it dirty," Diamond's silly ass said, not looking back. All the crack heads eyed Mac as they did everyone new, searching for any sign of weakness. So hopefully they could talk him out of something. The bottom floor of the house was being occupied by its owner Teddy. Ole' Teddy was a full blown crack head. He let Diamond rent all the rooms upstairs for some crack and a few dollars a month. Most of the clientele came from Teddy's spot. He'd turn them on to Diamond but most of the time he would end up copping for them and cuffing some of the rocks, then help them smoke what he had left. Teddy was a real shiesty character, if you weren't sharp he'd beat you before you could blink. Diamond had to beat his ass a few times until he got it understood that he wasn't no mark.

Diamond climbed the flight of stairs leading to the upstairs apartment, he fumbled with some keys then finally got the door open. "This is it," said Diamond waving his arms around at the shit hole.

"This is what?" asked Mac.

"It's the spot, the chill house, and your new home," said Diamond, as he flopped down in one of the leather recliners. As with any other crack house, everything was centered around the front room. There were two couches, a few recliners, coffee table, and a floor model TV with a VCR and a bunch of tapes stacked on it. Over in the corner sat a large stereo system and across from it sat a microwave on a night stand.

The rest of the house was pretty much neglected. Inside the bedrooms were box springs and a mattress with nothing else. The bedrooms were sometimes used by smoker's and that was only when they had a large bankroll and Diamond didn't want them to leave, so he'd let them use the back rooms to smoke until they were broke.

"Look, I gotta' bust a few moves young'in. I need you to hold the fort down. Huh," said Diamond, as he tossed Mac a sack of rocks. "That's five hundred right there, just give me four hundred back. Don't let nobody in except Teddy, and don't give nobody credit, not even him. I'm a come check on you in the morning and bring you something to eat. Oh, one more thing. If the police come just sit the rocks inside here," Diamond pointed to a hole on the backside of the TV. "You straight?" He asked.

"Yeah," Mac answered, eyes wide open and shaking like a leaf. He had been nervous since they pulled up, and now Diamond was talking about if the police came, and leaving him there by himself. This wasn't the deal. Or was it? Mac was having second thoughts as he walked Diamond and the girl to the door. He wanted to tell Diamond to just take him back to the Mission, but he didn't know what would happen if he went back, and he didn't want to look soft. It wasn't the pad he had imagined, but it was a roof and it wasn't the Mission. Mac locked the door behind them and leaned against it for a few moments trying to gather himself. He walked over to the living room and flicked the TV on, he flipped through the channels and discovered that they had cable. He didn't even have cable at his house, the spot didn't seem that bad after all. On top of the VCR sat a Super Nintendo game system and a rack of games. Mac turned on the system, grabbed a controller and got lost in a game of Mario Bros. Diamond knew how to get someone to stay put in the spot. Just have everything right there for them, and they wouldn't have a reason to leave.

    A knock at the door startled Mac. He paused the game and waited for a second knock. "Who is it?" He shouted trying to put some bass in his voice. "It's Teddy!" Mac walked over to the door and stood on his tippy toes trying to look through the peep hole. "What you want?" "Boy, open the door with yo' lil scary ass," Teddy snapped.

    Mac reluctantly unlocked the door and twisted the knob. Teddy barged in and walked into the living room. He stopped in the center of the floor and looked down at Mac. "Boy, this here is a business. Ma'fucka's be tryna' get they shit and go understand? So when I come up here don't be stalling and shit, understand?"

    Teddy was a very slim older cat, dark skin, with a bad case of tremors. He was always in a rush and for some reason expected everybody else to also be in a rush.

    "Boy, you hear me? I gotta go," He said walking in place.

    "Man, what you want?"

"Give me six for fifty."

"Diamond ain't tell me nothin about no deals."

"That's universal. You gotta' give a ma'fucka a play when they spending fifty or better."

"Tell you what. Wait till Diamond get back and he can give you a play."

Seeing that Mac wasn't biting. Teddy got frustrated. "Fuck it, come on with the five then. Shit," He said, trying to sound like he had an attitude.

"Money."

"What?"

"Where's the money? Diamond already told me yo' old ass think you slick."

"Ain't this a bitch? You lil' piece of shit. Here!" Teddy yelled shoving the fifty dollar bill in Mac's little hand. He'll try and fast talk a person hoping they'd forget to get the bread, but that was Mac's first lesson in the game. Always get the money first.

Mac handed Teddy five rocks and watched him closely as he examined them. "Let me see the other ones because these two are too small."

Mac reached down and pulled two rocks out of his sack, Teddy tried to swap them for the two rocks he had complained about but, Mac was on Game. "Man these ain't what I gave you,"

Mac said, then snatched the two rocks back.

"It's time for you to go," said Mac, grabbing Teddy by his shirt and leading him to the door.

"A'ight young'in, you caught me. I was just making sure you were sharp because you gotta' be in this game. What they call you?"

"Mac."

"Lil' Mac. A'ight my man. I'll be back here and there if you need anything just holla' down. If you need something from the store I'll make the run just look out for me from time to time."

"I got you," said Mac as he closed the door.

All through the night Teddy had been back and forth upstairs buying almost all of Mac's work. Mac had been up all night playing Mario Bros and Street Fighter, he hadn't so much as closed his eyes for a split second. He was totally unaware that the sun had come up and it was now morning. The traffic had slowed down. Teddy hadn't been up in a couple of hours. Mac had paused the game so he could run to the bathroom. As he flushed the toilet and was pulling up his pants he could hear a loud bang come from down stairs and then a lot of yelling. Mac thought that maybe the crack heads down at Teddy's were arguing or something, but then he heard stomping. It was the footsteps of the Wayne County Sherriff's Dept. Their raid team was racing up the stairs, and without warning they kicked the door in.

Mac's heart was pounding a mile per second. He stood frozen in the bathroom. "Wayne County Sherriff's!" They announced, as they searched each room guns drawn. A female Deputy bent the corner with her Smith & Wesson waving side to side, she jerked back at the sight of Mac. She closed her eyes and thanked God because she had almost pulled the trigger and would have blown Mac's head off. She holstered her weapon. "Got one in the bathroom!" She shouted. "Boy. What are you doing in here?"

Mac was still frozen solid. Other deputies joined the scene, one of them carrying the sack of rocks Mac left in the other room.

"Is this yours?" The deputy asked Mac, holding up the zip-lock bag of crack.

Mac shook his head no.

"Who's is it then?" The deputy quizzed.

"I don't know, it's not mine."

"What are you doing in here?" The female officer asked.

"Using the bathroom."

"No, I mean what are you doing in this house?"

Mac dropped his head and didn't respond.

"Are you living here?" The female deputy asked.

"Somebody probably got him up here selling that shit because they know juveniles don't get that much time," Another deputy added.

"Where do you live?"

Mac went into shut down mode. He didn't want nobody saying he snitched, so he kept his mouth shut.

"This is your chance to help yourself," said the female deputy.

Mac didn't budge. He ignored all their probing.

"Take his little bad ass downtown to the Detention Center. Bet he'll want to talk once them doors close and the judge sentence him to a group home," One of the deputies said, in a last attempt to scare Mac into talking.

They weren't bullshitting about taking him downtown. Mac was ushered into an awaiting raid van, and stuffed into the back seat, beside Teddy and two other crack heads. Teddy shook his head at Mac.

"How'd you let 'em find the product, youngsta'?"

Mac dropped his head into his chest, just as the back doors slammed shut, sealing them into sheer darkness. Moments later the van shifted into gear and lumbered away from the spot in enroute to the 1300 Beaubain 1st Precinct.

Chapter Six
Present Day

Mac walked out of Jackson State Penitentiary, with nothing but them stiff ass wrangler jeans on and that 50 dollars they give every inmate as their being released. He pushed back out into society   with nothing , an not only was he expected to survive, but miraculously somehow manage not to return.

He rode the Greyhound, perched against a window. His seat was in the back. A young, filthy white girl sat beside him, she constantly scratched and raked at her scalp, giving Mac the thought that maybe she had lice. Her stench testifies that she hadn't bathed. Could be worse, thought Mac. He'd smelled his cellmate's ass for nearly a decade, at least the ass he was smelling beside him was   a female and not another set of musty nuts.

Mac had learned to appreciate life and the freedom he'd been deprived of for so long. He laid his head against the window and took in the pasture of the country side.... After a while, he closed his eyes allowing his mind to wander with thoughts of what awaited him back in Detroit.

Since his first run-in with the law, Mac had been committed to the state of Michigan, and he'd been bounced around the juvenile system for years. By the time he got out of juvy, he'd lost contact with Los, ET, and Ebony. They were all grown up and away from the Mission. On Mac's latest bid, he'd caught a dime for a strong armed robbery turned bad. The victim bucked not allowing Mac to rob him without a gun, or so he thought Mac was unarmed.

Mac had set out to rob this old gay ass nigga name Blunt, who owned a liquor store in the hood. Blunt was also the brick man. He had a fetish for turning out young niggas, in exchange for putting them in the game. Mac caught the nigga coming out the store one night, and rushed him up against the wall of the store, basically on some strong arm shit, but Blunt began to tussle with Mac.

Two shots rang out, and Mac started running with nothing but the smoking 38. Special he'd popped Blunt with. The police caught Mac two blocks over on some hum bug shit. Cost him seven years.

Three years into his bid.... a letter slid under his cell door from Ebony. There was two pictures of her accompanied by the short letter, telling Mac that she never forgot about him, how much she missed and loved him, and that she'd ride out the rest of his bid, so long as God kept her above ground. She also told him that Los was getting money in Cincinnati and that ET was on a shit bag after being shot up.

Mac cradled a small photo album in his lap with pictures of him and the few comrades he'd met and grown to love and respect during his stretch. Along with the two pics of Ebony. She was still beautiful but Mac could see the hardships life had bestowed upon her in the lines of her face. She had told him, she was dancing and basically grinding however she could to survive.

She'd kept true to her word on holding Mac down, by sending $50.00 every two weeks, along with a short letter, which was more than Mac could have ever expected.

Ebony would be waiting on him at the downtown bus station. The plan was for Mac to stay with her until he got on his feet.

Mac had butterflies dancing around in his stomach, as he searched the many faces standing outside the bus terminal.... then he saw Ebony. Their eyes met at a distance, both their faces stretching into smiles, as they quickly closed the space between them.

Mac scooped Ebony up like she was a little girl. She pecked him on the lips, smiling genuinely happy to see him free. He sat her down and they hugged.

"I love you," Confessed Mac.

"I love you too," said Ebony.

She slipped under his wing, and they started walking toward the parking lot.

"I know you starvin'. What you want to eat?"

"For real," said Mac, looking up at the clear blue sky.

"I want a corn beef sandwich from Mr. FoFo's."

"Then, that's what it is," smiled Ebony.

They crossed the street and she slipped from Mac's grasp, as they approached a platinum 550 Benz coupe sitting on chrome. Ebony chipped the alarm. Mac slowed and stopped, taking in the car.

"Who whip?"

"Mine's. Ebony opened her driver door.

But Mac was still looking the car over... then his eyes settled on Ebony's fine frame. Her Coca-Cola bottle frame was adorned in expensive high-heeled boots, tight jeans and an expensive blouse. She also wore jewelry on her neck, wrist and ears, plus her hair was laid, fresh from the salon in a short do.

Ebony blushed, as their eyes met. "What?"

"Nothing," said Mac, as he walked around the car.

"No, tell me."

Mac held the door handle. "I don't know, but for some reason I thought you was out here struggling."

They both settled into the car and Ebony put the key into the ignition. Her wheels were turning as she pulled away from the curb. They rode off in complete silence.

"I was struggling.... until recently. When I, uh, when I met my new boyfriend."

Mac looked and listened to Ebony.

"Does he have a name?"

Ebony blushed. "Kevin."

"Well sis, I'm glad to see you happy."

Ebony's smile slowly faded, but Mac didn't notice because he had turned to the happenings outside his passenger window. The city is buzzing with traffic, con men, fiends, business people, ho's, killers and police.... Detroit.

"What you over there smilin' at?" asked Ebony.

"Just feels good to be back in the D."

"Well, it's good to have you back.... And after we leave Mr. FoFo's, we takin' you shopping."

Mac turned from the window, and Ebony tossed a bankroll of hundreds into his lap.

"What's this for?"

"It's for you, silly.... And there's plenty more where that

came from."

Mac unconsciously thumbs through the money, thinking that it had to be at least $10,000.

"Mac, I'm not lettin you get out here and do some bullshit that'll get you back behind bars, like the last time.... That's what that money's for. So you don't feel like you gotta' do the first thing that crosses yo' mind to get some money."

"Good lookin' sis,"

"No thanks needed. Just keep yo' butt free." Ebony reached for Mac's hand, giving him a loving squeeze.

Chapter Seven

Ebony and Mac stepped out of Broadway and City Slicker's with bags in each hand. They ended up spending $12,000. Ebony wanted Mac to look like the money he was destined to see, with her guiding him from the sidelines. Mac got fitted into three suits, with big block gators to match. Ebony assured him, that within two weeks time he'd be working with a full wardrobe, with minks to match.

After Ebony got Mac fresh, she took him to see ET, who had moved on the Westside with his baby momma. She nursed him back to health ever since he'd been shot up in a night club parking lot.

ET lived in the upstairs of a two-family flat off Linwood, an even shadier section of Detroit than the eastside, where he'd grown up.

When Ebony pulled up. ET was sitting on the porch nursing a 64 oz of Malt liquor, bare chested, with three nappy headed little boys playing in the dirt patched front lawn. ET's mask pulled back into a smile at the sight of Mac emerging from the passenger side.

"My ma'fuckin, nigga!" ET shouted.

"What up doe?!" Mac said matching his enthusiasm.

They meet at the stoop and embraced one another like the brother's they'd become back at the Mission.

"You been under that iron, I see." ET examined Mac from head to toe.

"You know a nigga gotta' keep his knock-out game in order."

"Shit'. These bitch ass niggas ain't fighting no more. You see me," ET pointed out his war wounds.

He hugged Ebony and kissed the side of her face. "What up sis?"

"You. How you been?"

ET looked at his boys wrestling in the lawn. "You know, just tryna' be around for my youngins."

"All them you?" Mac looked surprised.

"Yeah... Devin! Chris! Mac! Y'all come meet y'all's uncle."

Mac looked at ET, as the boys rushed over breathing hard and dirty from playing. ET rubbed them on their heads, introducing them one by one.

"And this my youngest boy, Mac. Y'all say what's up to ya'

uncle."

The trio said hello and gave Mac some dap, then ET allowed them to run off playing.

"You gave yo' son my name?" Asked Mac.

"I ain't know if I was ever gonna' see you again, my nigga. And I always thought of you as my brother. You and Los," said ET.

Mac looked at Ebony. "And you didn't tell me." Ebony just smiled. "Well, now you know."

"Y'all wanna' come in?" ET looked at the house.

Ebony turned towards Mac, wide-eyed. "Actually, we came to scoop you up. We finna' hit the new 007. Get this nigga some pussy, and get his dick sucked," said Ebony.

Mac looked at her in disbelief.

"What? It ain't like you had either in the last seven calendars. Shit', if it were me, I'd be tryna' get off first quarter."

"Sis, too raw, ain't she," laughed ET.

"Shit'. I know that dick hurt, unless."

"Unless what?" asked Mac.

"Unless you had a thang in there takin care of that,"

ET burst out laughing.

Mac laughed too. "Get the fuck outta' here."

"I'm just sayin.... it's 2019 out here."

ET headed inside the house, leaving Mac and Ebony play

wrestling.

"Okay. Okay. I was just playing," laughed Ebony.

Mac held her from behind. They were both smiling, as Ebony spun around, still within Mac's embrace. Their eyes met for a moment, it seem like neither one of them wanted to break eye contact until ET stepped down the stoop.

"Y'all ready?" asked ET.

"Yeah, we're ready," said Ebony, as she tore her gaze away from Mac, and sashayed towards the car.

Mac inhaled deeply, then released his breath, as he watched Ebony shift her hips and plush backside from side to side.

007 Strip club is located off 7 mile Rd and E Outer Drive. It's a shining post for every D. Boy and Jack Boy, who's currently at the top of their game. It's one of the top three exotic clubs in Detroit.

During the day time the club's crowd type, looking to buy a piece of ass during their lunch hour. Or there'd be a dope meeting being discussed at one of the tables. The real action didn't take place until well after eleven o'clock.

So Ebony, Mac and ET pretty much had the entire club and dancers to themselves. They had a section inside VIP with their table littered with an assortment of liquor shots and champagne bottles.

The DJ was spinning a mixture of all the latest hits, while

three naked strippers gave Mac, ET and Ebony lap dances.

Ebony had a mountain of dollar bills stacked on top of the table. She screamed out the lyrics to a Cardi B song and fanned bills over the women, then smacked one of them on the ass playfully.

"Welcome home baby!" she shouted over the music.

Ebony leaned over and whispered into Mac's dancer ear. The girl eyed Mac, while listening to Ebony and then a smile creased her face. Ebony pulled $500 out of her purse and handed it to the stripper. The girl grabbed Mac by the hand and led him over to one of the black leather sofas, pushed him down, then fell to her knees between his wide-spread legs. She quickly unfastened his belt and pants, expertly freeing his manhood. She massaged his growing erection from base to tip, while looking seductively up into his eyes.

Mac turned to see Ebony watching with a sly smirk on her face. Her gaze shifted to his nine inches.... just as the girl took Mac into her warm and moist mouth. He closed his eyes on contact and tilted his head back against the sofa.

The girl worked Mac over like the pro she was, sucking him like he was the last man on earth. Her deep throat game.... and the soft, tender way she held his pipe was sending Mac over the edge. He opened his eyes, only to see Ebony shamelessly enjoying the show. Her watching made Mac more excited as their eyes locked,

Ebony's pretty face fixed into a sexy smirk.

The girl popped Mac's dick out of her mouth and began jacking him off in a fast, short motion, concentrating on his head.

"Cum for me baby," she plead, in a sexy voice.

Before Mac could think, he was swallowed whole and shooting cum down the girl's throat.

She hummed and sucked harder with every burst of cum, jacking and milking Mac until he lay spun.

"Un-un. Get that dick back up nigga. I said head and pussy," Said Ebony, calling the shots.

The girl slowly stroked the length of Mac's manhood, while kissing the shaft, and stopping to suck his balls.... Mac found himself palming the back of the girl's head, as she engulfed him whole. The girl sat up, still jerking Mac's full erection. She accepted the condom from Ebony, who stood watching, as the girl used her mouth to slide the condom down onto Mac's dick.

Ebony bit her bottom lip seductively, and turned to leave as the girl straddled all nine inches of Mac. The girl rode Mac for at least ten minutes switching from front to reverse cowgirl, then gave it to him from the back.... Five deep strokes from the back and he was no more good.... He pulled out and ripped the condom off, then shot nut all across the girl's ass and up her back, without breaking eye contact with Ebony.

Ebony raised her champagne glass to her mouth and sipped, never taking her eyes off Mac.

Chapter Eight

After they left 007 Ebony dropped ET off, then headed back east to her ranch style home in East Pointe. The sun was just starting to set, as she whipped into the half-circular drive. A shiny black 760 BMW sat off to the side.

"You doin' it like that sis, two whips, big crib?" Mac said, as they parked.

"Naw, that's Kevin's car. One of his cars anyway."

Mac was slow to get out the car, and Ebony saw his apprehension. "Kevin doesn't live here with me, Mac. He just feel the need to leave a car over here. You know how y'all men are, wanna mark y'all's territory all the damn time."

Mac reluctantly got out the car, taking in the cool breeze and the tranquility the neighborhood provided. An older black gentlemen stood watering his grass next door. He gave Ebony and Mac a kind wave and closed smile.

"How long you been at this spot?" asked Mac, as Ebony

fumbled with her keys at the front door.

"About five months now.... come on," said Ebony, stepping inside.

She quickly decoded the alarm system, then kicked out of her boots.

"Welcome to my humble abode. My castle, is your castle. Make yourself at home," Ebony waved her hand before her, sheer luxury.

Mac took a step forward, taking in the state of the art kitchen appliances and granite counter tops. He followed Ebony into her sunken living room, where an enormous theatre style TV dominated the space. Plush crème sofas and expensive accessories made up the space.

"Take yo' shoes off and relax. I'm a freshen up a bit."

Ebony turned the TV on, then handed Mac the remote. She kissed his cheek, then headed off towards the back.

Mac called out after her, "Ain't you gon' show a nigga the rest of the house?"

"What part of make yourself at home, don't you understand. Don't get brand new on me. Yo' room to the right. Now, can I take my shower?" Ebony stood with her hands on her hips with that sly, sexy smirk on her face.

"Yeah, I'm good."

Mac watched as Ebony turned around seductively and purposely made her ass sway, with each step she took. She turned and smiled back at Mac, knowing he was watching her. He exhaled and shook his head, as she dipped into the bathroom. Seconds later shower water could be heard running.

Mac gave himself a quick tour, starting with the refrigerator, which was packed with fresh food, and the cupboards with everything needed to prepare a good home cooked meal.

His appointed bedroom had a king-size bed, two large dressers, walk-in closet, and a plasma TV. On the center of the bed sat a lone red rose and a small card, which read: Welcome home, Mac. Love Ebony xoxoxo.

Mac smiled at the endearment and took a seat on the edge of the bed. "I love you, too," he said just above a whisper.

Mac held his head down, lost in his thoughts. His thumb eased across the embroidery of the card. He sniffed the rose, and when he looked up there was a guy walking towards him.

Mac stiffened, as did the guy.

"Oh, my bad, dawg. I'm Kevin, Ebony's man.... You gotta' be her brother, Mac."

Mac accepted Kevin's extended hand, and they shook while Mac sized him up.

"It's good to finally meet you. She's been talking about you coming home for months now. I know you glad to be out of that bitch."

" Hell yeah."

"How long was you in there?"

"A lil' over seven years."

Kevin made a screw face. "Damn.... Well, you home now. If there's anything I can do, don't hesitate to ask bro I got you. Any family of Ebony's, is family of mines."

"That's what's up."

Ebony came walking up, dressed in a robe, still drying her hair with a towel. She slid under Kevin's tall, lean frame and into his arms.

"I see you two have met." She said smiling.

"Yeah, we good," said Kevin, kissing the crown of Ebony's head.

"A'ight then. I'm a turn in for the night. See you in the a.m. bruh," said Ebony.

"There's clean under clothes inside your dressers, holla if you need me," said Ebony.

"I'm straight. I'll see you in the morning, Lord willin," said Mac.

Kevin gave Mac some dap and Ebony winked at him.

"Good night, bruh," smiled Ebony.

Mac closed his door behind them, and began to strip out of his new clothes. His thoughts were stuck on Kevin.... it was too early for him to pass judgment on whether or not he liked the nigga. Seeing him with Ebony was already a strike against him, so the nigga had better turned out to be a show enough solid ma'fucka if he was ever going to win Mac's vote.

Mac climbed in bed, not bothering to pull the sheets back. His mind drifted to Ebony calling him bruh, and the implication he got from Kevin believing that he was Ebony's real brother.

Mac's thoughts were invaded by the soft moans of Ebony, along with the knocking of the head board in the next room.

"Oh, Kevin.... Ahh... yessss."

"Who pussy is this?"

"Ahh.... It's yours baby."

Mac laid on his back, eyes to the ceiling, blood boiling after listening to this nigga, and Ebony calling out his name.

The head board and moans ceased after about five minutes. "Ole' weak-ass nigga," said Mac.

Mac took a deep breath and tried to clear his mind so he could focus on more prosperous things, like his own game plan. He looked over at the $10,000 laying on the night stand beside him.... That was more than triple of what he had envisioned starting out with.

He knew that he only had one shot to take off, and everything he needed was right there in front of him. There would be no more fuck ups.... and going up the road for a stretch because he'd done some goofy shit.

I can't blow this.... not this time.

Mac told himself, that he would not have a sucka' attack over Kevin being Ebony's man. If the nigga was going to extend his hand, then Mac wasn't about to deny himself that much needed blessing.

He drifted off to sleep, with money on his mind....

Chapter Nine

Mac woke up in a cold sweat and wide-eyed, breathing hard... Ebony was at his side trying her best to calm him down.

"Mac, its okay... you're okay."

Mac took a deep breath, and began to settle down after realizing where he was... Shame overtook him at the realization, that his never-ending nightmares must've woke Ebony and Kevin.

Mac swung his legs to the floor and turned his back to Ebony. She understood, so she stayed with him, soothing his back.

"Mac, maybe you should see somebody," Ebony suggested in a small voice.

"For what, so they can get in my head and feed me some bullshit lies about how I should deal with it, when ain't no way to deal with it, Ebony.... Ain't but one way."

"And what's that?"

A long beat of silence lingered. Mac knew how to deal with his nightmares. In fact, he has been planning the perfect time and day to confront the man who had turned his already horrible life upside down... but first he had to get his money up.

"I'm sorry for waking you."

"Shhhh.... you have nothing to be sorry about Mac. I understand."

"What about Kevin, he heard me too?"

"Don't worry about Kevin. I'm your sister, and I got yo' back, knuckle head," Ebony playfully popped Mac in the back of his head.

"Ouch. What's that for?"

"Just in case you ever think about leaving me again," Ebony snuggled behind Mac, hugging him.

"You're stuck with me."

"Promise?"

"Promise."

Mac looked over at the alarm clock beside his bed, and saw that it was almost six o'clock in the morning, his eternal clock kicked in. Back in the Pen he would've been up and already out jogging on the yard. Sleep's a luxury, not afforded by the poor man on his grind, Pleasant CI would often say, just one of his many coined phrases.

Mac stood and kissed Ebony on the crown of her forehead.

"I gotta' get ready," he told her.

"Ready for what, nigga, you see what time it is?"

Mac laughed. "I know."

"So, what you getting' ready for, I know it's not a job interview."

"The takeover."

Ebony pulled back a closed smile and shook her head, as Mac slipped out the room.

He headed down into the basement, where he began his routine of calisthenics, jogging in place, burpees, Navy seals, squats, toe touches, and flutter kicks.... That being just the warm up. He went straight into his super-sets of push-ups and back arms.

The way Mac saw it, there wasn't no need in falling off after spending seven years building the body he'd worked so hard for. The way he saw it, the only thing missing was the money. Once he got some money, he'd be on top of his game on every level.

After finishing his work-out and showering, Mac helped himself to a hearty breakfast, cooking enough for Ebony and Kevin as well.

Ebony stumbled into the kitchen in a pink satin robe that bore her pretty legs.

"Boy, what is you doing?" she asked, taking in the scene of Mac working two skillets.

"It's been that long since a man cooked you breakfast?" Mac shot back.

Ebony rolled her eyes, as she sampled a piece of Western omelet. Her eyes closed, as she savored the bursting flavors.

Mac was cheesing from ear to ear, when she opened her eyes.

"Okay, you know a lil' some 'em,"

"Here," said Mac, as he pulled out a chair for her at the table. "Let me make you a plate."

"What y'all cookin', got it smellin' like a carry-out around this bitch?" asked Kevin. He stepped into the kitchen with a white wife-beater on and black pajama bottoms.

"Just a lil some 'em I picked up in the joint."

"Okay, well, let me see what you workin' with," Said Kevin, pulling out a chair.

Mac set them both out plates with omelets, pancakes, hash browns, wheat toast, butter, and sausage links. He fixed himself a plate and before long the only sound that could be heard were forks hitting plates and smacking....

"Dawg, you should open a diner or some shit," said Kevin, in between bites. "Shouldn't he baby?"

"Umm hmm," agreed Ebony.

"Naw, I just do it for the love of it," said Mac.

Truth be told, Mac learned how to cook long before he ever went to prison. Ms. Patty taught him how to cook most of her famous dishes. He mastered the ones he loved.

"So, what do you plan on doing?" asked Kevin, taking a sip of orange juice.

"I'm a secure the bag," said Mac.

Kevin nods in agreement. "Well, like I told you, anything I can do to help, just say the word."

"I just might take you up on that offer."

"We'll talk," assured Kevin.

"Mac is going to chill for at least a couple months ..," said Ebony.

But Mac cut her off. "A couple of months?"

"Yeah.... I mean, you've been gone for seven years, Mac. Do you know how much has changed since then? These nigga's ain't doin' time no more, they'll snitch on they own momma' before they go in. And you just gettin' out. These streets a eat you alive, there's so much snake shit goin' on. All I'm sayin', is give yo' self a fightin' chance by at least seeing what you up against because the rules you lived by don't exist anymore. Not with these niggas," said Ebony.

Mac was obviously flustered, but Ebony had not shot him down. A part of him knew she was right, and only looking out for his best interest. But then there was a part of him that felt he was ready to get to the bag, and waiting wasn't an option.

"I know you ready to put your million dollar plan in motion, but guess what ?.... ask me if I give a fuck? No, I don't because I meant what I said, Mac. I'm not finna' lose you again to the pen or to the grave. Do you hear me?"

Kevin rose with his plate and glass in hand, stepping over to the sink, providing them with some privacy.

"Mac, look at me," said Ebony.

Mac looked Ebony in her eyes and saw the love of a friend, family, and then some.

"I'm a take my time, sis."

"That's all I ask. For you to take your time because I promise that shit ain't goin' nowhere."

Chapter Ten
Two Weeks Later

Mac exited the Secretary of State with his driver's license, something he had never had in his entire life. Ebony made a deal with him, that if he got his license, she'd give him the titles to the burgundy Maserati sitting inside her garage. It was a gift from Kevin, but she never drove it because she hated convertibles.

Ebony was parked outside in the passenger seat of the Maserati, with her window down, she smiled as Mac strolled outside.

"Tell me something good," said Ebony.

Mac smiled, holding up his temporary paper license. He had taken the test twice before, failing, and making three times a charm. Mac climbed behind the wheel of his new car, then adjusted his seat and mirrors.

"I told you, you could do it," beamed Ebony.

"I ain't gon' lie, if I ain't pass that shit this time, I was finna' say fuck that."

"Mac, we're grown out this bitch, and doing more dirt than a lil' bit."

"So?"

"So.... We gotta be legit, even when we're doin' dirt because that's the only way to balance the shit out."

Mac put the car into drive and looked over at Ebony. "You know you done turned into a damn philosopher on me," laughed Mac.

Ebony playfully shoved Mac "Boy, bye. You should be glad I'm lacing yo' boots to this shit out here."

"I am, baby girl, you know I'm just playin wit you," smiled Mac, as he pulled into traffic.

"Well, I'm not. Mac, I want to see you make it... and part of making it, is you have got to last...."

Mac was digesting Ebony's words, as he drove with one arm stretched out to the wheel....

Ebony continued. "You'll never guess how long Kevin's been in the game."

Mac looked at her for the answer.

"Twenty years. And guess how many times he's been to jail, fuck prison?"

"None, Mac. And you know why? Because he has mastered

the art of lasting out here. But guess what else, Kevin ain't doin' nothin' that you can't do. But it's all on you."

She had Mac thinking, especially after she compared him to Kevin. Ebony was trying to get Mac to see, that the game and life was about longevity, not going in and out of prison and starting from scratch each time out.

"Take me home. I know you wanna' enjoy yo' new ride." Ebony offered a weak smile.

"I'm enjoying it now."

"Me too, but I promised my hair stylist I would help her plan this hair show."

"You gon' be in it?"

"Yessss," said Ebony, batting her eyes.

"Look at you, model, entrepreneur.... Any other hidden talents I should know about?" joked Mac.

"Maybe," answered Ebony, her eyes dreamy and sly, sexy smirk.

Their eyes held for a beat, with Mac turning away first. He couldn't stand looking into her eyes for more than a moment.... it was as if she could read his mind, and if she could he didn't want her to see how bad he wanted her.

Ebony reached for the radio and cranked up the volume to Jay-Z featuring Mary J. Blige, Can't Knock the Hustle...

Ebony sang along to Mary's part, smiling and dancing in her seat.

She turned and sang this part to Mac,

"Baby, one day you'll be a star...."

Chapter Eleven

Mac let the top down on the Maserati, as he came up off the Davidson Expressway. He was stopped at the light on Linwood, when a shiny blue Lexus pulled alongside him. The fine red bone behind the wheel had the top back, Mac's eyes settled on her angelic face cloaked in big designer shades, her hair at a natural shoulder length curl. She cradled a small dog in her lap. Her thick yellow thighs bust wide open.

'Damn she bad,' Mac thought. But, as soon as he was about to say something the light changed and she sped off. ' If I ever see yo' lil fine ass again I'm mashing the gas.'

Mac made a right turn onto Linwood, then cruised down the block, drawing stares from the young hustlers and a few little kids.

ET was sitting on the porch with a pint in his hand. His ugly mug stretched back into a smile as Mac pulled up.

"Okay... I see you, my nigga," said ET.

"Come on, let's slide," Mac said. He had no intentions on

getting out.

"Bae, I'm gone!" ET bellowed out, then made his way to the car.

"Where the fuck you get this pretty ma'fucka at?" Asked ET, as he slid into the Italian leather.

"Ebony gave it to me when I got my L's"

"Damn nigga! She blessed the shit outta' yo' ass."

Mac pulled away from the curb and headed towards the expressway.

"Let's hit Belle Isle," suggested ET.

"That shit still be jumpin'?"

"Nigga, you know The Rock always jumpin'."

Mac smiled at the memories of ET, Los, Ebony and himself hanging out on Belle Isle AKA 'The Rock'. They called it The Rock because it's an actual island, which sits off the Detroit River, and is connected to Detroit by the bridge. The summer time is when people from all over Michigan go there to hang out on Belle Isle. Car clubs, teenagers, cook-outs, reunions, whatever. The Rock's open to all.

Mac turned off Jefferson Ave onto the Belle Isle Bridge.... he felt good being free, with his brother, ET at his side, a pocket full of money, and a brand new foreign whip. Two weeks ago no one could have told him that his life would've been what it was at that moment. He was blessed to have Ebony in his corner.

They made it onto Belle Isle, blending in with the moving traffic. Several cars were packed with young females looking for a good time, likewise there were even more cars packed with men, young and older looking to hook-up.

"Say, ma! What's good with ya'll? Pull over!" shouted ET, hanging out the car, pint still in hand.

The car full of girls laughed and kept on driving.... ET flopped back into his seat pissed.

"Fuck them raggedy ass bitches."

Mac couldn't help but laugh, same ole' ET.

ET turned up the rest of the E&J he'd been nursing, then chunked the bottle into the softball field.

"Damn, we should've grabbed somethin' to drink," said ET.

"We can swing back through if you want."

"Naw, it's cool."

ET fired up a Newport, then scanned the faces standing outside their vehicles, some people were playing their sound systems. The younger crowd was posted up drinking and smoking. They were obviously politicking with the opposite sex.

ET took a long pull from his cigarette....

"So, what's the plan, my nigga? We ain't really chopped it up since you been home."

"Shit', that's why I scooped you up. We need to put somethin' together."

"Shoot."

"I wanna' open a trap around there where you stay and a couple more spots on the eastside."

ET pulled hard on his cigarette, then flicked it out the window.

"Ain't no money sittin' in no spots these days, my nigga. Nigga best shot at gettin' rich is outta' town, and then comin' back when you got yo' weight up."

A beat of silence passed.

"Why you think Los stay gone? Because he done figured out ain't no real money in the city, not when a nigga competing with a million other niggas, and everybody got the same shit."

"Why you ain't go out there with Los?"

"I got a family now, Mac.... And to keep it a hunid' shit ain't the same with Los."

"What chu' mean?"

"You'll see."

ET had Mac's wheels spinning... what could have happened between ET and Los while he was on lock, that things weren't the same?"

"Bruh, let me ask you somethin," said Mac.

"What's up?"

"Ebony's out here havin' her way, and she ain't hit yo' hand with nothin'?"

"Naw, you know how she is, bruh. I mean, she looks out by hittin' me with bread when I'm fucked up, but she ain't tryna' plug a nigga on the work."

Mac had a realization, as he thought about the $10,000 Ebony gave him, the car, along with all her pep talks about taking it slow.

"She got that lame she fuckin' wit, soft-ass nigga eatin, bruh. He seeing no less than fifty of 'em. And sis won't put a nigga in the game," said ET.

"Let me work on that. And in the meantime, I want you to pick us out a spot around yo' way. It ain't what you sellin', but how you sellin' it. That alone gon' be the difference between us and everybody else."

"You know I'm with you, bruh."

"And that's all I need."

Mac and ET dapped up. "Now, let's go get that drink," said Mac.

Chapter Twelve

The next day Mac waited at the house until he heard Ebony leave out for her hair appointment. Mac had been trying to catch Kevin on the low, so he could take him up on that offer he promised when Mac first came home.

Usually, Kevin would've left out either with Ebony or early morning. But today he was running late. Mac was waiting in the living room, as Kevin headed for the front door.

"Mac, what's up with you my baby?"

"Shit, you. I was tryna' holla' at you before you hit the road."

"Talk to me."

"I'm ready to open up shop on the Westside. Trust me, it's plenty of money flowin' through that bitch, but I need..."

Kevin cut Mac off, "You need some work?" A smile creased Kevin's face, as he took a seat on the arm of the sofa.

"Yeah, but you also see how Ebony been on my ass."

"She loves you, Mac." He paused "These past few months,

you was all she talked about."

"And I got nothin' but love for her too. But as a man, I gotta' make some moves. I need my own spot, you feel me?"

"I feel you, which is why I'm a bless yo' game. All I ask, is that you keep me in the clear with yo' sister. I ain't gave you nothin, you feel me?"

"What's understood don't need to be explained."

"Well, listen my nigga. I don't sell nothin' under ten bricks. But I'm a put two of them in yo' life. Don't worry about payin' me back right now. Flip as many times as you can, and in 30 days take care of me on the back end. Yo' ticket gon' be eighteen-five."

"That's love."

"Love on my end. Loyalty on yours. Stick wit' me, Mac.... and I'm a make you a millionaire in six months."

"Love and loyalty," said Mac, extending his hand for Kevin's.

They shook on it, then Kevin raised to his feet. He looked at his watch.

"Well, let me get up outta' here. I'll have that for you in about an hour. Just keep yo' phone on,"

"A'ight bet."

Mac let Kevin out and leaned against the door for a moment, envisioning his rise in the game. Everything was coming together for him, now all was left up to him. He had a fleeting thought of Ebony, then told himself, she won't find out.

Chapter Thirteen

The first thing Mac did once Kevin hit him with the two bricks was rent a nice two bedroom apartment behind Eastland Mall. He not only needed a spot to call his own, but a stash spot that no one knew about. He had too much respect for Ebony to bring anything illegal into her domain. He knew she'd be apprehensive about him renting the apartment, which is why he told her only after he'd signed the lease and paid the deposit.

"Well, I guess so," said Ebony, rolling her eyes at Mac.

They were standing inside his bare living room, Mac with his arms wrapped around Ebony's waist.

"You gon' come visit me?" he asked.

"We'll see. You need to let me decorate this place for you."

"If that'll cheer you up, then yeah." Mac rubbed his nose against hers.

"You make me sick," she blushed.

"You know you love me."

"I do," confessed Ebony.

A beat passed with them sharing intense eye contact. Then a smile enveloped Ebony's beautiful face.

"What?" Asked Mac.

"Remember when we first met at the Mission? I use to give you a hard time every chance I got"

"Of course I remember.... I remember seeing you for the first time and thinking to myself. Damn, shorty the prettiest girl I ever laid eyes on."

Ebony twisted her lips up in disbelief, "Boy, bye, run that game on somebody else."

"I'm for real."

"Then why you ain't never say nothin'?"

Mac took a deep breath and exhaled, then looked away. He searched for anything other than the truth. Ebony sensing his apprehension turned his face so that their eyes meet.

"Why?"

"Because in the beginning you was so damn mean , and by the time we got cool, I just started looking at you. I guess how Los and ET look at you."

"And how was that?"

Mac frowned. "Like family."

Ebony smiled. "Good, because that's how I see y'all, as my

family. And I wouldn't do anything to ever jeopardize that."

Mac searched her eyes for any signs that she was holding back... then he realized that maybe she wasn't, and maybe she meant what she said.

Chapter Fourteen
The Come Up

The two-family flat ET had them set up shop in was perfect in location, as it provided easy access for all their customers and a birds eye view of any signs of the raid team. The flat sat on the corner of Linwood, four houses down from ET's flat, but on the opposite side of the street.

Carleta was an old neighborhood crack head, she'd been smoking since the days of free base, and had graduated to shooting speed balls. But yet, her drug of choice was still crack cocaine. She owned the flat, and reminded her tenants of her lordship every time her pipe was empty. Her frail bag of bones stayed dressed in house clothes, with her hair wrapped up in a once elaborate scarf, moving from the top apartment, down to the first floor flat with impunity out of not wanting to miss a hit.

Crack heads from as far as the suburbs would gather at Carleta's in search of a place to cop and smoke, while others looking to barter as much as sexual favors in exchange for that get-high.

Mac was just the latest dope boy to rent out the top flat.... Carleta was a force to reckon with, she'd rent out the top flat, then go back on her terms as soon as her pipe went empty. Her heart was full of larceny, something ET had forewarned Mac about going in. But the way Mac saw it, if he could make a good two week run, he'd be up and any stunt Carleta might pull wouldn't mean much because they could just move the operation and the clientele would follow.

The work Mac got from Kevin was A-1, he was able to cook two bricks from one, and the fiends had no qualms.

To separate himself from all the other dope boys slinging dimes and twenties, Mac opened shop selling double-ups. Whatever a fiend spent with Mac, he was doubling them up. Usually, only a hustler on the come up would give double-ups, but Mac had changed the game. To him, it wasn't about how many kilo's they could move. The ends would justify the means, Mac told himself, as well as ET, who didn't like the idea of giving away free product to fiends.

But all doubts from ET went out the window their first day in operation. Word had spread, that some Eastside boys had them double-ups around at Carleta's. The traffic commenced first with the local crack heads, having to see and test the product themselves. Once the local's gave their stamp of approval, those same die hard fiends began pouring in the money, turning their suburb clientele onto the spot, all the while brokering each transaction. It was a win for everybody.

Carleta's pipe stayed packed, the locals were skimming off the top, and Mac was watching his dreams come to life with every ounce that him and ET chopped down into dimes, twenties and fifty pieces.

"Nigga, I told you," said Mac, looking over at ET.

They were standing at the kitchen counter, each with plates and razors, chopping rocks.

"Yeah, this bitch shakin', bruh. But this a lot of damn work. We been cuttin' this shit up all day."

"That's part of the grind, my nigga. Shit. We could still be walkin' around here with our hands in our pockets, waitin' on somethin' to fall through."

ET remained silent, he just nodded his head in agreement.

"All we need is two weeks of us puttin' in the work ourselves, then we gon' put workers in the spot. That way we can move around, and open up more spots. All around the city. Same shit, double-ups."

"I'm wit chu', my nigga," assured ET.

That first day they moved almost a whole brick in double-ups. With the low ticket Kevin was giving Mac the bricks for, along with the quality, Mac was able to do his double-ups, and still see a comfortable profit in the end off of every kilo. His goal was to have the spot moving nothing less than two kilo's a day. Once word spread throughout the city, he was convinced they'd start meeting that 2 kilo a day quota.

Chapter Fifteen

It had been two weeks since Mac and ET opened up shop at Carleta's and everything was moving like a well-oiled Machine. ET had finally been allowed to hire two young hustler's, Swift and Nando. He had them coming to the trap in shifts as if they were working a normal 9 – 5 job. Meanwhile, Mac was on the other side of town doing his part. He was scorching and searching the area until he located and hired two sister's Tiffany and Tenell to cut up crack for eight hours. Everybody worked in eight hour shifts.

Less than a week later, Mac unsurprisingly met his quota of moving 2 kilo's a day, and he did so by making an even bigger demand for his double-ups. He had Carleta and the locals spread the word, which his spot would only operate from 10:00 a.m. - 8:00p.m. And once the spot shut down for the night, it was a wrap until the next morning.

What ended up happening was the spot had two main rushes, like a heroin spot. One in the morning when the spot opened, and another before eight o'clock. Not to mention the midday traffic buzzing through the spot.

But as expected everybody was not happy with Mac's success... He was blowing up, but at the expense of the other dope boys. Think about it, you have to put yourself in their shoes. If Mac and ET was pushing that much work in pieces the other hustlers were taking a drastic pay cut. And anybody with half a brain would know that, that would piss off the competition.

"Fuck them Eastside niggas," A young dark skin dude shouted out the window of a off white Chevy Tahoe.

Most of the thugs in that area were born and raised on the same corner they were watching Mac and ET get rich on and to add insult to injury Word was spreading fast. Everyone was beginning to talk about the two Eastside niggas that were fucking it up on the West side.

Mac and ET had been standing on the porch, on a number of occasions and saw this champagne colored Seville slide through, with an ugly ass black nigga in it mean mugging the spot.

"Dawg, who the fuck is that nigga?" asked Mac as he watched the Seville turn the corner.

"That's Black Aaron's hoe ass. Nigga got a spot around the corner. He keep slidin' through here because he know all his licks shoppin' with us now."

"Yeah. Well, I ain't feelin' the way he keep looking at us. He act like he want some smoke or some shit'."

"He can definitely get it. What's up?" asked ET.

"I'll let chu' know."

Mac turned to ET and folded his arms over his chest.

"What's good?" asked ET.

"I think we don' took the spot as far as we can take it, and it's time to expand."

"I'm listening."

"I'm a try my hand on the eastside. You know, open up a few bandos. I want you to keep this shit runnin' though. Yeah, leave it just like this and we gon' be partners. Nothing will change, fifty-fifty split straight down the middle."

ET broke into a wide shit eating grin, and extended his hand for Mac's. They embraced with a half-hug.

"Time to turn this shit up a notch," said Mac.

"I got chu, my nigga" assured ET.

They ended the embrace and separated.

"I got an idea, let's go out tonight. Kinda like a celebration of what's to come," said Mac.

"Shit. You know I'm wit' it. You think we should invite Ebony?"

Mac considers it for a moment, then shrug.

"Fuck it, why not. We'll get up later, say about nine, cool?"

"A'ight, that's a bet."

Chapter Sixteen

Ebony was throwing all of Kevin's clothes out onto the front porch and lawn, when he pulled up in his black on black 500 Benz.

"Here nigga, take all yo' shit and get the fuck outta' my house!" yelled Ebony, still slinging articles of clothes.

Her neighbors were much older than her and Kevin, but they weren't being shy about watching the drama unfold on their otherwise quiet street.

"You making yo' self look like a fool out here," Kevin growled, then glared at the old man next door.

"No, Kevin. You've made a fool out of me. I ain't never let a nigga make me a side bitch. And to think this whole time I thought you were my knight in shining armor. But, in real life you ain't shit!" She paused for emphases. "What the fuck was you thinking? Huh?!" She stopped him before he could utter another word. "Shut up bitch! Ugh. You just like the rest of these niggas."

Ebony slapped Kevin so hard that his face turned to the side.

"I'm done playin' the fool. Go home to yo' wife and kids."

"Baby, let me explain."

"Nigga, didn't I say go home to your wife!"

She screamed as loud as she could and spat between Kevin's eyes. That's when he lost it completely. He cocked back his arm and hit her with a punch intended for a man, straight in her face.

Ebony yelped, and instantly put her hands up to her nose, then looked at the thick blood spreading through her fingers. Tears began to stream down her face, more so out of anger than fear.

"Bitch, I'm a kill you!" screamed Ebony.

Kevin had a glimpse of remorse and regret in his eyes, as he shook the pain away in his hand.

"I'm callin' the police," announced the old man next door.

Kevin looked to Ebony once more, then turned to leave.

"You put yo' hands on the wrong one bitch! I got chu'!"

Kevin waved her off, as he slipped behind the wheel of his Benz. Ebony ran into the yard and grabbed a brick from her flower bed. She crashed the brick into the windshield as Kevin was backing out. He gritted his teeth, but put the car in drive and sped away, leaving Ebony falling to her knee's crying and banging her fists into the ground, as she watched the tail lights of Kevin's Benz disappear.

Her next door neighbor, an older black woman named, Ms.

Ruby cut across their bushes and knelt beside Ebony, consoling her.

"Come on, baby. He's gone.... It's going to be alright. Come on, let's go inside and get you cleaned up," offered Ms. Ruby.

Ebony was crying hysterically, but Ms. Ruby did manage to help her up and get her inside the house where Ms. Ruby stopped the bleeding, and put an ice pack on Ebony's head.

Ms. Ruby laid Ebony across the chase lounge inside the living room and took a seat at the edge of the chase.

"Chile, ain't no man, God made is so good, that they're worth lettin' em put they hands on you."

"But I shouldn't have spit in his face," said Ebony in Kevin's defense.

Ms. Ruby tapped her leg. "No, you shouldn't have, but that still doesn't excuse him hittin' you like a damn man."

Ebony looked away in thought. "He's never hit me before."

"And if you leave 'em now, he never will again."

Ebony had a look of uncertainty. She loved Kevin, even with him and all the lies he put her through.

"Love's a dangerous game." said Ms. Ruby.

"You ever loved someone more than you loved yourself?" asked Ebony.

"Chile, yeah." A memorable smile arrested Ms. Ruby's wide pretty face. "A few times actually." Her smile lessened and she dropped her head, lacing and unlacing her fingers. "You should never give someone else that kind of power over you. They'll only use you up."

There was a knock at the door, then it pushed open. "Police! We got a call about a disturbance."

Ebony looked to Ms. Ruby, uncertain what she should do. The police slowly entered the house and found Ebony and Ms. Ruby in the living room.

The white female officer nodded at the blood stained shirt of Ebony to her male partner.

"Ma'am, who did this to you?" asked the male officer.

"I don't want to make a report or nothin'," said Ebony.

Ms. Ruby gave her a sad look as she stood to her feet.

"We want to put the person away who did this to you, so that he doesn't do it to anyone else," said the female officer.

"Really, it's not a big deal. We just had a small fight, and it looks worse than it was," said Ebony, trying to convince herself, more than the officers.

The officers looked at each other, and then the young white male shrugged.

"We can't force you to press charges. But if he comes back and assaults you again, promise me that you'll call us?"

Ebony gave him a meek nod.

"Okay, you ladies have a nice evening, and please be safe." said the female officer.

Just as the police showed themselves out, Ebony's cell phone chimed.

"I should get going then," said Ms. Ruby.

"Thank you for looking after me," said Ebony.

"Anytime," Ms. Ruby winked.

She let herself out... and Ebony lifted her phone off the coffee table as it chimed again. She stared at the screen.... it was Mac calling. She couldn't talk to Mac, he'd hear it in her voice that something was wrong, and he'd be on his way back to prison once he found out Kevin had punched her in the nose. Ebony sighed, letting her voice-mail pick up.

Tears started streaming down Ebony's face. She loved Kevin, and thought that he was the one she'd someday marry and start a family with. But here it was, he already had a family. A wife and two kids. Ebony was heartbroken to know that she wasn't nothing more than a side piece and replaceable.... She had to wonder how many other side pieces Kevin had stashed away in nice suburban homes, pushing fine cars and taking exotic trips on the whim.

But even with all his trifling ways Ebony couldn't bring herself to say she'd never see Kevin again. Maybe he wasn't happy with his wife, she told herself. And maybe he'd leave her in due time. Ebony told herself, that just maybe she should've heard Kevin out.

Chapter Seventeen

Mac stuck his phone into the console after getting Ebony's voice-mail. He was speeding down Jefferson Ave with the top down, ET in the passenger seat. They both were dressed to the nine's in slacks, blazers, gators, and Rossellini's. A BYOB function was being held at the Fox, and the dress code was for Bosses and Playa's only.

"She still ain't answering?" asked ET.

"Naw, she probably sleep or already out with Kev."

"Yeah, probably."

When they pulled up to the Fox, it was like a red carpet event, but at the Playa's Ball. Bad Bitches were everywhere, dressed in sexy numbers and heels. Every sack chaser and Boss Bitch was in attendance.

Mac parked at the curb, looking like they belonged, as the gleam of the Maserati turned some heads.

ET took a moment to appraise and appreciate a few asses

passing by before falling in step with Mac. They entered the luxurious lobby and paid the admission, then followed the traffic into the main ballroom, where elaborate tables were set up as VIP an open bar, and a cleared out hardwood dance floor. Mac and ET stood under the entrance a moment just soaking in the scene, before taking it over to the bar.

"What can I get y'all." a sexy red bone bar maid asked.

"Shit." ET looked to Mac. "Give us two bottles of Mo'"

She smiled and turned for the cooler, then came back with their bottles of black labeled Moet.

"There a hundred each," she informed.

ET balled up his face, but Mac quickly intervened, by producing the money.

"Thank you." said Mac.

He and ET ran away from the bar, checking out the action.... Beautiful women were at every corner. The women out numbered the ballers by ten to one, easily. And they were still pouring in.

Mac caught the eye of this pretty brown skin chick seated at one of the tables across the room. She was with three of her girlfriends, and all of them were bad in their own way. But Mac was taken back by Pretty Brown Skin.... maybe it was the fact that she was openly flirting with her eyes. Mac could tell that she was thick and sitting on an onion by her thick thighs showing under the table.

"Baby girl, checkin you out, my nigga." said ET.

"Yeah, I see."

"So, go put on, and put an ugly nigga in the car wit' one of her girls," shot ET.

"I got chu', just chill."

Mac turned around and summoned the sexy barmaid. He whispered something to her, while eyeing the ladies table across the floor.

The barmaid retrieved two bottles of Don P. and put them in ice buckets, then personally carried them over to the ladies table. She nodded in Mac's direction , and all the ladies broke their necks trying to see who had sent the bottles over. Mac raised his own bottle in acknowledgment, and the Pretty Brown skin bitch he'd been eye-fucking pulled back a wide pretty smile.

"A'ight, nigga, now go over there. They on a nigga dick," said ET, in a hushed voice.

Mac took a drink from his bottle, then sat the bottle behind him on the bar. The DJ was spinning a record by the group NEXT.

Mack pushed away from the bar and cut across the floor headed for the ladies table. The women saw him coming and whispered to each other, while Pretty Brown Skin blushed.

"How y'all ladies doing tonight?" asked Mac, as he approached their table.

The dark skin one with short hair, smiled and said, "We're good. Thank you for the bottles."

"Oh, y'all welcome," said Mac, looking at the one he came for. "Do y'all mind if I borrow your girl, what's yo' name ma'?" asked Mac.

"Seven," the young lady answered in a soft, sweet voice that did something to Mac.

"Shit, she grown," Her sexy yellow bone friend spat, raising her glass to her full pout.

Mac extended his hand, and Seven obliged by accepting his reach and raising to her feet. Her body was thick down to the ankles.... Mac was taken aback by her beauty and stature.

"Come on, let's hit the dance floor," said Mac, guiding her away from the table.

"Okay, Miss Thang," One of her girls called after her.

NEXT's hit was still pumping when they made it out to the dance floor. Seven wasn't shy about her curvaceous body, not at all. She fell into the music and Mac followed her lead, when she turned around and backed that plush, soft ass against him.

Just as the song went off, now girl, I know you felt it... *But boo, you know I can't help it. You're making it hard for me...*

Seven looked back at Mac with a devilish smirk just as the female sang, *step back you're dancing kind of close... felt a little poke comin' through... on you.*

They mixed it up and danced for two more songs. Mac was feeling Seven's vibe. She was fun to be with... her spirit was beautiful. He was attracted to her beyond just her banging body. There was something in her eyes that held him captive every time she looked at him.

"So, are you going to tell me your name?" asked Seven, as they left the dance floor.

"They call me, Mac."

Seven stopped and put her hands on her hips.

"What?" Asked Mac.

"I am not callin you, Mac."

"Why not?"

"Because that is not what your mother named you, and besides.... I want to get to know you."

Mac had to respect Seven's honesty. No one had even questioned his name before. Only one person in his life ever called him by his government, and that was Ms. Patty.

"Ramon." "But everybody calls me, Mac," he insisted.

Seven broke into a pretty smile. "Well, I like Ramon better. And you'll get to know I'm not everybody else."

"We'll see." said Mac, sizing her up.

"So, that means you gon' give me yo' number?"

Mac rucked his brow.

"What, you ain't use to a woman who goes after what she wants?"

"Can't say that I am," confessed Mac. "At least not when it comes to men."

"Well, when I see somethin' I want, I got after it, and more often than not, I get what I want."

Seven looked deep into Mac's eyes....

"Let me buy you another drink," suggested Mac.

They headed over to the bar, where ET was trying his spiel on the bell pepper body runt next to him. The beast was smiling and blushing at ET's every word...

Seven smiled and asked Mac, "Isn't that yo' friend?"

Mac laughed it off. "Yeah."

The sexy barmaid brought Mac a fresh bottle of Moet without asking. "And what will it be for the lady?" She asked.

"I'll have a Moscato," said Seven.

The barmaid went off to fix Seven's drink.

"Are you just getting out?" asked Seven, out of nowhere.

Mac's head snapped back in shocked.

"I'm sayin', you got this glow that I only see on guy's who just came home. Your eyes and skin are clear. Yo' lips ain't all black from smokin' weed and you got a nice build."

"You see all that, huh?" Mac took a swallow from his bottle.

"So, am I right?" Pressed Seven.

"You're very observant, I'm a say that much. You sure you're not the law." said Mac jokingly.

"Actually, I am..."

Mac's eyes narrowed.

"Kinda, sorta of. I'm a PO. I use to work in corrections, so I've seen a thing or two."

Seven sensed this was a problem for Mac, maybe even a deal breaker.... The barmaid slid her drink to her, then faded down the bar.

Seven looked to Mac.... but his eyes seemed to have lost all interest, as he looked across the room at nothing in particular.

Seven grabbed her drink and meekly took a step back. "Thanks for the drink. And for the dance. I'm a go check on my girls."

Mac simply nodded, as he watched Seven turn and walk away. He hated all law enforcement the same. Especially CO's and Po's because they'd always scream how they weren't the police when called so, but yet they kept a nigga in cuffs. Mac didn't trust no bitch with a badge.

Too bad, he told himself, watching the sway of Seven's phat ass. ET's locked the fat chick's number in his phone and made his way back up to their section.

"What's up with baby girl?" asked ET.

Mac turned away from the bar. "That bitch police."

"Word?" ET looked at Seven. "So what though?"

"ET, one thing I know about them police ass bitches. As soon as they get mad at a nigga all that police shit come out of 'em. Won't be me." said Mac.

"Damn." said ET.

"But what about you? I seen you gettin' at big baby."

"She got that check bruh. Bitch own a chain of checker's and Rally's."

"You gon' cuff 'er?"

"Am I?" smiled ET. "Make her big ass pay like she weight."

ET downed the rest of his bottle, then tapped Mac. "Let's take some pictures, my nigga." ET grinned, and then nodded towards the camera man and his set up.

"Naw, I don't be takin' no pics, my nigga."

"Mac, how else the world gon' know we was ever here? When niggas talk about us twenty years from now, we want 'em to be able to back our stories with the pictures."

"ET, you drunk," laughed Mac.

"Naw, I'm good. All I'm sayin' my nigga is, it ain't no sense in us getting all this money, getting fly, and being scared to take some pictures. The whole time you was in the pen, I know it was other niggas showing off they pics of them balling."

Mac nodded.

"They wasn't just sho' boatin'. They was livin' through they pics, their good memories. The shit that kept reminding them that they wasn't always at the bottom. And that they could go to the top again one day."

"You wanna' take some pics?" asked Mac, jokingly.

"Come on," said Mac, leading the way.

Mac definitely felt ET and everything he said, although the whole time he'd been locked up he never looked at it the way ET had just broke it down.

The picture man had a background of down town Detroit's skyline, along with dollar signs rising like smoke up into the clouds.

Mac and ET posed with fresh bottles of Moet, and on one picture they embraced by holding hands and staring into the camera. In all, they took five pictures, Mac promising to give one to Ebony when he saw her.

As they were cutting across the floor, an old school player seated at a table stopped Mac.

"Say, young playa, what's yo' name?"

"Why? Do you know me?!" Mac scowled.

"Naw, but maybe we should fix that."

Mac looked at ET, who was on the ready as always. The old head picked up on the vibe. "It's not like that, Mac, my man. They call me, Solomon." The old timer was clean, dressed to the nine's and even without the fine clothes he reeked of money. Old money.

"Have a seat, if you will." Solomon a short dark man, he waved his manicured hand at the empty chairs around the table.

"I'm a be at the bar," informed ET.

Mac took a seat. The table was full of buckets of champagne, yet Solomon sat alone.

"Where you from, Mac?"

"Eastside."

"Eastside boy, huh? I'm from Schafer myself, but that ain't never limited me to just that small corner of the world." Solomon was sizing Mac up in a God fatherly type of way.

"You drinking?" Solomon waved a hand over the table.

Mac raised his own bottle. "Thanks."

"Right." the whole time he'd stopped Mac, Solomon hadn't stopped smiling.

Mac didn't know if that was just one of his characteristics, or what.

"Mac, I'm a good judge of character, which is why you're sittin across from me, and not all these other young wanna-be hustla's... Look around, they know who I am, and any one of 'em would suck a mule's dick to be seated where you're at right now."

"So, what's up?" Mac cut through the chase.

Solomon chuckled a bit, then nodded. "I like you already, Mac. Straight business. You keep that same attitude and you'll maybe go as far as me in this game. Take my number and call me on Monday."

Mac rucked his brow, but he fished his phone out anyway and said "Give it to me."

Solomon read him his number, then Mac stood up.

"Use it now." smiled Solomon.

Mac simply nodded, then made his way back over to the bar, where ET nursed his bottle.

"What that old nigga talkin' about?"

"Shit. Just gave me his number and told me to call 'em Monday."

"You gon' fuck wit' 'em?"

"I don't see no need to really.... We already got the plug we need, feel me?"

Chapter Eighteen

The next day Mac needed to re-up, so he called Kevin, but he kept getting the operator, telling him that the number was not correct.

Mac was pacing back and forth in ET's basement, phone in hand... ET was at the table with their re-up money spread across the table.

"What's up?" asked ET.

"Dawg must've lost his phone."

"We missin' money like a ma'fucka. We ain't got no work."

"Shit. We ain't missin' nothin'. Where else they gon' get our double-up's? We just gotta' wait, and so do the fiends."

ET sparked a cigarette. "How about we cop a half from my man until dawg get right?"

Mac thought this over for a moment.... He wasn't ruling it out, his only hang-up was he couldn't be certain the work was anywhere as good as Kevin's fish scale. Kevin was serving the streets the same way he got the work, untouched.

Mac looked at the time on his phone, then tried calling Kevin one more time. He shook his head at the sound of the operator.

"Fuck it, hit cha' man." Mac tossed ET his cell.

"I gotta' go upstairs for the number." said ET.

Mac continued to pace the floor. He could only hope things were still good with Kevin, and that he only lost his phone or maybe changed his number. Mac knew not to call Ebony, inquiring about Kevin because he didn't want to tip his hand. But he told himself that he was going to check on her anyway. As soon as they got things back in order.

When ET came back downstairs, he was ending his call with his connect.

"A'ight, he said twelve thousand, bruh," said ET.

"Damn, this nigga taxin'. I thought you said this was yo' man?"

"I been knowin' Cease for a minute. Dawg on the team wit' some money gettin' niggas, but he eating off the back end. You know how that shit be."

Mac wasn't trying to hear about all that, he didn't know this nigga Cease. The nigga was trying to hit them over the head.

"What chu' tell 'em?" asked Mac.

"I told 'em to come through, and bring that.

"A'ight, fuck it. As long as the shit straight, we gon' grab it just this one time though."

Cease pulled up in a fire engine red Vette on chrome. Big fat and black nigga, about 260 and tall with it. Cease had a menacing look on first sight, but he was soft as baby shit, just a big ole' Teddy bear.

Down in the basement, Mac sized Cease up, as ET made their introduction.

"What up doe?" Asked Cease.

"Shit, tryna' get right," said Mac, getting straight down to business.

"I got chu' together right here." Cease pulled the half-kilo from his waist, handing it to Mac.

ET was rolling a blunt over at the table.

"Y'all can use the kitchen over there," said ET.

Mac found a glass and filled it with water. He scooped a finger tip of the cocaine into the water, and watched as it dissolved into a cloud. If it wouldn't have made any bubbles or rose to the top, Mac would've known that it was badly stepped on. An old school test he picked up on back in the day from watching Damon cook up.

"It's a'ight," admitted Mac.

But it still wasn't what Kevin had been blessing him with. Mac gave ET the nod to pay Cease, while he went straight to the stove with the entire half-brick. Using just a big metal pot, Mac dumped the coke into the pot, added barely enough water to cover the coke, then he set the fire on medium, until the coke began to cook. That's when he started feeding the cocaine with baking soda.... He stirred the mixture then waited before adding more soda.... He fed the coke until he saw that it couldn't be fed anymore. That's when he added the ammonia, the final touch.

When Mac finished whipping the work, he had brought back 26 ounces. That was enough for them to make it through the rest of the afternoon, and hopefully the evening rush.

Carleta had her pipe ready as soon as ET and Mac walked inside the door.

"Where it at? I smell it," said Carleta, spitting because she didn't have her teeth in.

"Here you go, Hit that shit, then put the word out that we back on," said Mac.

Carleta tested the product, which didn't garner any rave reviews by her. "What happened to that other shit?"

Mac looked at ET and shook his head. If Carleta peeped the shit was different, then how many other fiends would complain. Mac knew deep down all of them would have gripes because that's just how good Kevin's shit was. Anything else was a down grade.

"That shit ain't nothin, Auntie?" ET asked Carleta.

"It ain't what chu' had, that's for damn sure."

"Let everybody know we back on," said Mac.

One bad batch wouldn't ruin everything they worked to build, Mac told himself. As soon as Kevin hit him off the fiends would be right back to serving him like their god. He just had to get up with Kevin.

Chapter Nineteen

After leaving ET to hold down the spot, Mac decided he'd stop by and surprise Ebony. And he was hoping to see Kevin as well. All the fiends were mildly complaining over the change in product. Mac needed that A-1 if he was going to hold his clientele.

When Mac pulled up at Ebony's house her car was parked in its usual spot, but no sign of any of Kevin's cars. Mac still had a key, so he let himself in. The house was quiet, with the exception of the TV coming from the living room.

"Sis, you home?!" called out Mac, as he slipped off his shoes.

The bathroom door opened and Ebony stepped out into the hallway. "Hey, bruh." her tone was low and meek.

"What's wrong wit chu'?" Mac closed the space between them, instantly inspecting the dark rings under her eyes. He lifted her chin, but she shied away. "Eb', who did this to you?"

"It's nothin', don't worry about it."

Mac's blood pressure rose to a million. "Fuck you mean, don't worry about it?! Kevin did this to you?" Mac made her look into his eyes.

"We had a fight, and I..."

"Naw, fuck that." Mac turned away from Ebony.

"Don't make no excuses for this nigga," he told her. Mac punched the wall hard, shaking the mounted pictures, and startling Ebony.

Thinking out loud, Mac said, "That's why his soft-ass changed his number. Ole' bitch-ass, nigga."

"How.... how you know Kev changed his number?"

"I ain't never lied to you, sis, so I ain't finna' start today. He was helping me get on my feet out here."

"You went behind my back, Mac, I can't believe you." Ebony stormed off into the living room.

Mac followed her and sat close to her on the sofa. He fixed the loose strands of hair on her ponytail, while she sat with her arms folded, and staring at the TV commercial.

"Eb', you know I ain't mean to upset you... I was just tryna' get on my feet as a man. My bad for keeping that from you."

A beat passed without either of them saying a word.

"You gon' stay mad at me?"

"I ain't mad. I just wanted you to take yo' time, Mac. I keep tryna' tell you, that this money ain't going nowhere, and neither is the penitentiary."

"Eb', I'm not going back to prison for nothin'."

Ebony snapped. "I hate it when you niggas say y'all ain't never goin' back."

"I'm not."

"And what you gon' do, snitch this time?"

Mac felt like Ebony had just slapped him in the face, that's how much disrespect he felt.

"I'm a act like you ain't just say that stupid shit to me." Mac chuckled and shook his head.

"What the fuck you gon' do that's guaranteed to keep yo' ass outta' jail?"

"I'm a hold court in the streets." said Mac, in a flash of anger.

"And what about me, huh? You gon' just leave me again.... And what I'm suppose to do, huh, Mac? Oh, I get to bury your ass, huh? All that time you did, and you ain't learned shit I see."

Ebony had Mac 38-hot.... She had pulled his card and saw right through his ass. His plan was about as typical as the rest of the low level dope boys around the city.

"But you know what, since yo' ass wanna' jump into that fire so bad, I'm a put you in play."

"What chu' mean? I ain't fuckin wit' that nigga, Kev no more after what he did to you."

"Fuck Kevin. I was with Kev because I love 'em and thought we'd be together. But that lil' money he playin' wit' ain't nothin' out here.... I'm a put you on how he wish he could be plugged." said Ebony.

Ebony hadn't heard from or seen Kevin since their fight, and it was enraging her to think of him playing house with his wife and kids, like what they had never existed.

Ebony had larceny and payback in her heart. She was cooking up a revenge that would dethrone Kevin, and have him crawling at her feet, begging that she take him back.

"Let me make a call." said Ebony.

Chapter Twenty

Ebony had fixed herself up to leave the house, hiding her black eyes under makeup and big designer shades. She hadn't left the house since her fight with Kevin.

She was behind the wheel of her Benz, with Mac in the passenger seat. They drove back into the city in silence.

Mac couldn't wrap his head around the way Ebony had just talked to him. He questioned whether she was wrong or right. Her bluntness had always been her best attribute. She had no filters, her pair of lips would say anything to anybody. Mac knew Ebony was just being herself.... and deep down he knew she only had love for him.

As far as what she said, Mac had told himself many of dark lonely nights laying in those prison cells, that he'd die before ever going back to prison.

Mac took a deep breath at the thought of dying out there on the cold streets of Detroit. He was looking out the passenger window.... said faces and turmoil was all he saw in each passing soul. Mac told himself, that he'd die too before he saw himself living the way the passing faces were, struggling, broken, and just existing.

Ebony pulled the Benz up to a tattered bar in Southwest Detroit called Sheeba's. Mac was looking at the place and at the fiends and crack whores passing on the side-walk.

"Come on," said Ebony, reaching for her door.

Mac followed her to the front door of the bar, where she barely rang the buzzer before the door swung open.

A massive black nigga, every bit of 6'8 and all muscle stood in front of Ebony. He slowly moved aside, after hearing the go ahead from the bar.

"Bull, let her in! She good!"

The bar was empty, with the exception of Ebony, Mac, Bull and the old head standing behind the bar smiling.

"Hey, baby girl," the old man spat.

Ebony sat her clutch down and leaned over the bar to kiss his cheek.

"Hey, daddy. You lookin' good, as usual?" smiled Ebony, as she slid onto a stool.

"I'm makin' it, what can I say."

The old head jerked his head at Mac. Bull sneered, then

took a seat at one of the tables, and resumed his after-hour drinking session.

"Daddy, this Mac. Mac's like a brother to me," said Ebony.

"You were at the Fox the other night?"

"Yeah," acknowledged Mac. He recognized the old head. "Solomon, right?" asked Mac.

Ebony looked at Mac with her brow raised.

"Yeah, I gave you my number.... see how thangs work themselves out?"

Mac nods solemnly and takes a seat beside Ebony

"What cha'll drinkin'?" asked Solomon.

"I need a strong shot of Tequila." said Ebony.

Solomon looked to Mac.

"I'll take a Corona," said Mac.

Solomon busies himself retrieving their drinks, but still making conversation.

"So, what's the plan, baby girl? Talk to me." said Solomon.

Ebony looked at Mac. "I want you to fuck with my brother. I brought 'em to you because I know he ain't poison first of all, and I know you can take 'em where he's tryna' go." said Ebony.

Solomon sat their drinks down in front of them, then he pulled a Mike's Hard Lemonade from the cooler, and twist the cap. All the while, he hadn't stopped smiling. Solomon took a swig from his bottle and the smile was gone, as he met eyes with Mac.

"I don't' do nothin' less than fifty keys at a time," said Solomon. He was watching Mac's response.

"What's the ticket?" asked Mac.

"Since its baby girl bringing you to me.... I'm a let you get 'em for fifteen." said Solomon.

"On consignment?" asked Mac.

"Do you need consignment?" asked Solomon.

"For at least the first couple runs," admitted Mac.

Solomon took another swallow from his bottle. He looked at Ebony and nodded, then pulled back his patented million dollar smile.

Ebony knew then that it was a go.

"Come see me tomorrow around this time, and I'm a have yo' order ready." said Solomon.

"Appreciate you fuckin' wit' me." said Mac.

"Like I told you the other night, there's a lot of nigga's right now wishing they were in your shoes. Just make good on it." said Solomon.

"Thank you, daddy." smiled Ebony.

They kicked it a little while longer, then Ebony and Mac said their good-bye's to ole' Solomon. On their way out, Solomon pulled Ebony to the side, while Mac used the bathroom.

Solomon pulled Ebony close by her waist and she giggled like a little school girl, as he kissed around her neck.

"When am I going to see you again?" asked Solomon.

"How about this weekend?" Asked Ebony.

"Okay. Saturday we'll take the yacht out, and I'll have you all to myself." whispered Solomon.

Ebony blushed and put her hand to Solomon's chest, making some distance when she heard the bathroom door open.

Solomon whispered to Ebony, "and don't think I can't see those two black eyes."

"I'm okay," assured Ebony.

Mac walked up and Solomon extended his hand.

"A'ight now, see you tomorrow." said Solomon.

He let them out, slapping Ebony's ass out of sight of Mac. Ebony smiled back at him, but kept her stride.

As they pulled away from Sheeba's, Mac had a thousand questions racing through his head, but the number one question was how did Ebony know this nigga, Solomon?

Ebony's mood had seemed to pick up. She was still smiling, and yet she and Mac hadn't said a single word to each other since leaving the bar. As she got onto the express way her favorite song by Jay-Z featuring Mary J. Blige came on. She reached for the volume, and broke out singing the chorus:

"Who do you think you are?".... Looking at Mac and smiling. ...*"Baby one day you'll be a star...."*

Mac turned the volume down and Ebony looked at him as if he were crazy.

"What's wrong wit' chu'?" asked Ebony, with much attitude. "Shit."

"Sis, where you know this old ass nigga from?"

Ebony balled her face up. "Solomon? I been knowing him for a few years now. Why?"

Mac looked out his window.... and his thoughts were fleeting. He really didn't know why it mattered how Ebony knew Solomon.

"What difference does it make Mac how I know Solomon?" "He's about to put you on. Hell, you about to take this shit to a level you ain't never seen before. But like he said, don't blow it because an opportunity like this only comes once in a life time."

Mac nodded, as Ebony reached for his hand and laced their fingers together. When he looked at her she had that million dollar smile of hers going, that was always a pleasure to see because she rarely gave it up.

Chapter Twenty-One

Mac stayed a little while with Ebony once they got back to her house, but he told her that he had to get going, but promised to check up on her in a couple of days. He forewarned Ebony though about Kevin.

"If I catch that nigga over here again, I'm a bust his ass on sight."

"I'm done with him." said Ebony, not sounding to convincing.

"You better be." Mac kissed the crown of her forehead, then stepped off the porch. "Call me if you need me."

"Love you. Be careful." called out Ebony.

When Mac pulled up to Carleta's flat a crowd of people were gathered at the side-walk. But they weren't just crack heads trying to score and keep it moving. Mac recognized many as neighbors and his years of being in the Pen had taught him how to read body language. And the way people were looking and huddled into whispers, it told Mac something was definitely wrong.

Mac parked across the street and searched for any sign of ET.... But all he saw was Carleta standing at the top step of the porch, hands on her hips, with her hair a usual mess and her face balled up.

Mac caught the bullet hole through the front windows of the downstairs living room, and the closer he looked... the more bullet holes he picked up on. The house had been sprayed.

Mac's heart skipped a beat. *Where you at, my nigga.* Mac dialed ET's number and sunk back into his seat while the line began to ring.

"What up doe?" Answered ET, on the second ring.

Mac exhaled in thanks. "Dawg, where the fuck you at?"

"I'm at the crib. I need you to pull up."

"I'm down at the spot." said Mac.

"I'm on my way."

Mac slid his phone into the console, and he saw ET jogging across the street in his side view mirror.

ET opened the door and eased into the passenger seat. Mac pulled off as soon as ET was inside. A lone police car was pulling up to Carleta's just as Mac turned down the side street.

"What the fuck happened?" asked Mac.

"Two nigga's call they self, first tryna' rob the spot. But

Nando peeped the move and started bussin' first. The nigga's bust back but took off runnin'. They came back like ten minutes later and shot the downstairs up."

"That sound like more than a robbery. Sound like a nigga tryna' put us outta' commission."

"I bet chu' it was that bitch-ass nigga, Black Aaron," said ET.

"Who?"

"The nigga in the Seville who keep ridin' through mean-muggin'. Nando said the lil' nigga's be pushin' work out of one of Black Aaron's spots."

"Oh yeah."

Mac knew what was required in a situation like this. The streets was watching, and the wolves thought they smelled blood. Mac wasn't no nigga's vic or prey. A demo had to be put down for disrespect, and to let the streets know that they'd bust they gun too.

Mac thought about the 50 keys he was supposed to pick up from Solomon the next day. He knew once they got to playing with that kind of work there would be many more demo's to follow.

Mac sighed...

"What's wrong, my nigga?" asked ET.

The truth was Mac felt himself being sucked into the ills of the game. The money and power was what everyone wanted, but no one wanted everything else it took to maintain the money and power. Every day, there would be a new contender trying to knock you off so that they could take your place. Mac was built for it.... he just knew the end result would either be a casket or back to prison for life.

"We gon' bag this nigga tonight." said Mac.

Mac could have easily told ET to handle it, and it would've been taken care of no questions asked. But Mac was cut from a different cloth, the one where a man doesn't ask someone else to do something, he wouldn't do himself. And this was as much Mac's problem as it was ET's, so Mac felt obligated to be the one that put in the work.

Once night fell, Mac and ET went around to ET's crib and they suited up in all black. ET had always kept an arsenal of guns. He loved guns more than anything. Down in the basement ET laid out a spread of assault rifles, on the table.

Mac selected a SKS with two drums.

"I call that bitch, Gorilla Nuts," said ET.

He cradled a custom stock AR-15. They both checked the chambers, and ET stuffed two extra clips into his hoodie.

"We out." said Mac.

Mac wasn't on no shoot a nigga house up and maybe kill an innocent by-stander, or worse a kid over some bitch nigga's sins.

Mac was an up close and personal nigga when it came to beef and the murder game. He didn't want it to be no mistake about it when he got his man, who it was meant for.

ET had stolen a Dodge minivan. Mac was laid across the back seat, while ET drove around in search of Black Aaron, or the two nigga's who had shot up the spot.

"That nigga usually be up at the store around this time." said ET.

They eased passed the liquor store, both scanning the store front and parking lot, but no sign of Black Aaron. His car wasn't parked outside his crib, so ET knew it was just a matter of time before they ran into him. Black Aaron was the typical nigga, he lived and breathed only Linwood, which meant he hadn't went too far.

ET's eyes lit up when he saw Black Aaron's burgundy Caprice sitting in the Coney Island parking lot. The inside of the restaurant was well lit.... Black Aaron and the two shooters were all standing around the counter talking to the young black woman behind the register.

ET made the first turn off and rounded back.

"They in Coney Island, my nigga," said ET.

"I got 'em." said Mac, getting ready.

"I'm a hit Aaron hoe ass..."

"Naw," said Mac, "Just pull up to the door, and keep the

engine runnin'."

"But what about..."

"I got 'em, trust me, my nigga," said Mac.

ET didn't like the idea of Mac going alone because there was three of them, plus he knew they had to be strapped. But ET did as Mac said, by pulling the van up to the door of Coney Island. It was a one way in, one way out spot. Bullet proof glass separated the workers from the open sit in area.

Two young girls sat at a table off to the side. While awaiting their orders. The girl's eyes bucked in fear at the sight of the hooded figure busting into the door, rifle in hand.

Black Aaron was the first to turn around, and the first one to get hit. Mac hit him four times before his body hit the ground. The other two nigga's tried to scramble and reach for their waists, but they didn't stand a chance. Mac drilled both of them with a series of shots to their torsos. Mac stood over them one-by-one, issuing head shots, saving Black Aaron for last.

When Mac ran out of Coney Island a thick cloud of gun smoke hung in the air, and the two young girls were screaming at the top of their lungs, as was the black woman behind the register.

Mac dove into the back seat of the minivan and ET sped off. He jumped the curb and peeled away from the scene.

"You hit them bitch ass niggas!" yelled ET. He was amped,

as they sped away.

Mac pulled back his hood and looked down at the SKS in his lap. "It's gon' be a few more niggas we gon' have to put down." said Mac.

Chapter Twenty-Two

The nightmares had been lying dormant for about a week or so since the last time Mac woke up haunted by his mother's dying eyes. The murders on Black Aaron and his underlings must have done something to trigger Mac's nightmare of his dead mother, because he woke up in a cold sweat and breathing hard, as if he had just escaped from being killed himself.

Mac rubbed his face, then looked over at his alarm clock on the night-stand. The sun was already up. It was a quarter after seven o'clock in the morning. A fleeting thought of what took place the night before flashed through his mind, but Mac blocked it out. He sat up and snatched the sheets from his cold sweaty body, then headed for the bathroom and took a shower....

When Mac finished showering, he dug through his stuff he carried out of prison. He was looking for Burch El's information. Although he didn't make any promises to Burch El, Mac fucked with him on a genuine level, and since he was up at the moment he felt it only right to send his comrade a smile.

Mac stopped at the Western Union and put $1,500 on Burch El's books. He knew that would make him smile, and he'd know Mac was doing alright. The way Mac saw it, he was paying homage to a fallen comrade, and in doing so just maybe he, himself could escape the ills of the game, even if it was only temporarly.

Mac still had a few hours to burn before it was time to go see Solomon. He drove all through the Eastside of Detroit into the neighborhoods, seeking out potential spots he'd set up in the near future.

Mac then found himself in his old neighborhood before he knew it, he was driving down his old childhood street. His palms grew sweaty against the steering wheel, and his breath was caught in his throat, as he approached his old house.

His mother's dead eyes flashed before him, as he looked toward the house she was brutally murdered in. Mac squeezed his eyes shut at the sound of her faint voice. His foot stabbed the break causing the car to skid to a stop dead center of the street.

When he opened his eyes two little girls playing in Ms. Patty's old yard were looking at him. Mac wondered a bit if the girls were any relation to Ms. Patty.... then he drove away feeling embarrassed by the scene. He couldn't bring himself to look through the rear-view back at the house. He made the first turn onto Robin Hood, then drove back up to 7mile.

Mac pulled up to Al's Barber shop and parked behind the big body Benz out front. He used to get his hair cut at Al's back in the day. Every two weeks, Ms. Patty would send him to see Al, so he could get his hair cut.

Mac doubted if anyone inside the place would remember him from back in the day. But that was fine with Mac, at least he was returning at the top of his game. He told himself as he stepped through the door and all eyes were on him, 'that they'd definitely remember him next time.'

Mac nodded to old man Al and the other three Barbers, then took an empty chair amongst the others waiting to be cut. Two old timers slapped checkers against the board, while talking plenty of shit to each other.

Gossip filled the air, and clippers hummed, just the way Mac had remembered Al's. The Channel 7 local news was playing on a mounted plasma screen. No sound was coming from the television. It was on mute. The reporter was standing across the street from Coney Island, where Mac and ET caught Black Aaron slipping the night before. As the reporter pointed toward Coney Island, the camera zoomed in on the yellow crime scene tape.

"Damn, fools out here," said Al, catching the captions on the bottom of the screen.

The reporter explained how three targeted men were ambushed and killed last night inside the carry-out. Witnesses reported seeing a hooded figure armed with an assault rifle. The camera equipment inside the eatery was inoperable at the time, explained the reporter.

Mac relaxed now that he knew, he was in the clear. The screen flashed pictures of the deceased, with the reporter adding that Black Aaron was wanted for questioning in a string of homicides, and that Detroit Police were calling this retaliation.

Mac waited his turn, passing on the other barbers until Al's chair opened-up. Al's barber shop was a cornerstone in the neighborhood. And Al, himself was a boss playa on many levels. He wasn't just a barber. He was a hustler, real estate investor, old-time pimp, a therapist to his clients, and a father-figure to the neighborhood kids who sat in his chair once or twice a month until they reached adulthood.

As Al popped his cape and put it around Mac's neck, he eyed Mac with a sense of familiarity.

"You use to come in here when you was a boy?" asked Al, as he fastened the cape.

"Yeah." answered Mac.

"It's been some years. What's ya' name?"

"Mac"

"Yeah, sure.... I remember you."

Mac wondered how much ole Al remembered about him....

He was hoping it had nothing to do with his mother.

Chapter Twenty-Three

When Mac pulled up to Sheeba's bar, Solomon's body guard. Bull was standing outside smoking a cigarette, while another older man stood with his back turned hunched over a barbecue pit.

Bull wasn't the social type.... he eyed everyone with the same amount of suspicion, and he issued out equal violence at the word of Solomon. Bull looked at his watch as Mac climbed the curb, then snatched the door open, allowing Mac to enter. "He's waiting on you," informed Bull.

Solomon was standing behind the bar watching the lottery numbers roll out. "My man, Mac," said Solomon, as the last number rolled out.

A heavy-set woman was seated at the bar, she had been scribbling down the mid-day numbers into a small notepad. "I'm a check the numbers for today." she told Solomon, then gathered her pad and drink.

Mac needed no explanation to see that Solomon was also

running numbers. It was an old school, and also full proof hustle. Every old nigga with a bankroll seemed to have tried running a policy, as the streets called it, or numbers. Mac could only hope to live as long and to see as much money as Solomon.

"Can I get you somethin'?" offered Solomon.

"Naw, I'm good. But thank you."

Solomon waved a hand for Mac to come around the bar. Mac followed him into the kitchen area and into the freezer, where a mountain of wrapped kilo's sat against the wall. Opposite of the cocaine was an arsenal of weapons.

"That's a hunid' of 'em. When you're done with the first fifty, these will be waiting on you."

Mac tried his best to keep it G. He had never been around that much work in his life, and Solomon sensed it. He patted Mac on his shoulder and said to him. "You'll do fine... Just always remember to never let your right hand know what your left hand is doing... And always keep your word, huh?" "You might want to pull around back, so you can load these into your car," said Solomon.

Mac nodded and found his legs moving him out of the freezer. He didn't know what he was thinking by not having a better vehicle in place to move 50 bricks across town, let alone not having an official stash house in place. Mac realized then, that talking about 50 bricks, versus seeing them was two different things. He realized the first thing he needed to do was to find a better safe house then his apartment.

Mac pulled his Maserati around to the alley of Sheeba's and he loaded the 50 bricks into his trunk as quickly as his limbs allowed him to. Solomon offered no assistance.... He stood aside smiling as he always does, watching Mac work himself over.

When Mac stuffed the last five kilos inside the trunk and slammed it shut, Solomon's smile vanished, and he closed the space between him and Mac. Looking Mac seriously in the eyes, he warned. "Remember what I said about keeping your word. You're not the first would-be hustla' Ebony's brought to my door-step. The last one ran off owing me, Mac. Shame what I'm a do to 'em when he turns up. Because they always gotta' come back for somethin."

Mac squinted his eyes at Solomon. He didn't take kind to threats, if that's what this was.

"Luckily for the both of us, Solomon. I'm into doing good business, you feel me?"

"Yeah, I feel you."

"But I'll let you know if anything changes on my end."

A smile creased Solomon's old ugly face, as he watched Mac slip behind the wheel of his Maserati and drive down the alley....

Mac stared back at Solomon through the rear-view until he made the turn out of the alley. Mac couldn't help but wonder who else Ebony had turned onto Solomon and if the last nigga had taken flight on him, then why was Solomon trusting him with 50 bricks?

The first thing Mac did when he made it back on the Eastside, he leased a storage garage right there on the spot and he unloaded 45 of the kilos into the storage unit. His next stop was a used car lot, where he bought a conversion van that was fairly new with good mileage. He would use the van strictly for transporting the work from Solomon's bar to his storage unit. Mac paid the Arab who owned the lot an extra $3,500 to equip the van with two sealed stash spots large enough to store 200 bricks if need be.

By the time Mac got the van situated, ET was calling him repeatedly...

"What up doe?" Answered Mac.

"What's good, my nigga? I been tryna' catch you all day."

"Had to get straight, you feel me?"

"Oh, so we good then?" ET was elated.

"I'm on my way to see you."

"A'ight, in a minute."

Mac had one brick underneath the battery of the Maserati as he headed for the West side. His plan was to show ET everything from scratch, how to whip the work into two bricks and turn over the spot to him like they had planned before all that shit with Kevin and then Black Aaron popped off.

Mac could still hear Solomon's warning, about not letting his right hand know what his left hand was doing. This included ET.

When Mac made it to Linwood, ET was sitting on the porch nursing a pint of Hennessey and smoking a Newport. His little boys were out in the yard wrestling. Mac pulled into the driveway and up to the side door, where he popped the hood. ET helped him retrieve the brick from under the battery, then they entered the house through the side door and down into the basement. They headed to the kitchen area.

"Guess what?" asked ET.

"What's up." said Mac.

"Los hit me when we got off the phone. He on the road on his way back to the city."

"Word?" asked Mac. He was genuinely happy that he'd get to see Los.

"Yeah. And the nigga sound like he got some money 'n shit. That's the only time he come back to the city, so he can stunt, then go back outta' town."

Mac didn't care about that shit. "Did you tell 'em, I was home?"

"Naw, I thought we'd surprise 'em."

"Good." smiled Mac.

Mac busted open the kilo and grabbed a Pyrex pot from the

cupboard. He ran the water in the sink, while ET stood over his shoulder.

"Now, I'm a show you this shit here one time, so pay attention."

"A'ight," agreed ET.

Mac walked ET through the step-by-step process on how to stretch good cocaine into double, using just water and baking soda. Mac didn't feel like ET was ready to whip an entire key at one time, so he showed him how to whip nine ounces at a time out of 4 1/2 ounces. The plan was they'd split the profits down the middle, and Mac would keep ET with the work he needed to run the spot.

Mac stood aside and watched ET whip up the second 4 1/2 ounces.... ET had it down. He brought back 9 ounces just as Mac showed him. They dapped up, with ET cheesing from ear to ear.

"Los wouldn't teach me this shit for nothin' in the world," said ET.

"Naw?"

"Nigga didn't even want me in the kitchen watchin'."

Mac laughed. "He probably needed you to look out."

ET shook his head.... "Naw, my nigga. Los wanted everything for his self. You'll see."

This wasn't the Los that Mac remembered from back in the day. Not the same Los who had given him a brand new track suit when they didn't even know each other. Los was the one taking care of the crew, and he was the one who turned them all out to the game. Now ET was saying he changed.

Chapter Twenty-Four

Mac ended up pulling an all-nighter fucking with ET, helping him cut up the rocks for the morning rush at the spot. After that though, Mac told ET that he was on his own, and he needed to hire some more help because the sisters had quit.

Back on the Eastside Mac stopped at the Diamond Glow $2.00 car wash on 7Mile & Mt. Elliot. The Maserati needed a wash, but that wasn't the reason Mac turned into the car wash. A young nigga in a clean cutlass Supreme with gold 22" rims was standing near his whip, while two worker's applied Armor All to his tires. Mac figured him to be no older than 17 maybe. He had a sense of style about him, and Mac could tell the young nigga was in the streets.

Mac made eye contact with the slim yellow nigga, as he pulled around to the entrance. The young nigga was eye-fucking the Maserati because it wasn't the average hood car. Most of the niggas getting money in the city would either be in a Benz or BMW.

That Pitch Fork symbol meant at least $150,000 or better.

When Mac pulled out of the automated wash the youngster was still outside his car talking on his cellphone. Mac pulled beside him and got out so his tires could be hit with Armor-all.

The youngster ended his call and his eyes immediately fell on the gleaming Maserati.

"That bitch hard, yo," said the youngster.

"The Cutty's holding it's own." said Mac, giving the youngster his props.

The youngster looked back at his car with a smile. "Thanks."

"What they call you?" asked Mac.

"Dae Dae"

"Mac." said Mac, extending his hand.

They shook hands and Dae Dae went back to admiring the Maserati.

"Let me ask you somethin'," said Mac.

Dae Dae looked at Mac. "Sup?"

"You hustlin'?"

"Yeah, I get my hands dirty. I got a couple spots, why what's up?"

"Here, take my number."

"What is it?" Dae Dae asked, then pulled out his cell phone.

Mac gave him the number and told him to call tomorrow

around noon.

"Bet," said Dae Dae.

He watched Mac slid behind the wheel of the Maserati and pull out of the car wash. Mac had big plans for Dae Dae, and every other young hustler on the rise. Mac had decided the best and fastest way to move 50 bricks on a consistent basis, was through the hands of other mid-level hustlers. Dae Dae said he had a couple spots. Mac figured he was probably copping 9 ounces or less. But Mac was going to put a brick on him, and help him get his weight up. Because the more money Dae Dae saw, the more Mac would see.

Mac spent most of his morning scouting for young hustlers. He had taken a page out of ole' Solomon's book. The same way Solomon took chances on believing in up and coming hustlers, Mac figured he'd do the samething. All the while following his advice of not letting his right hand know what his left hand was doing. Mac would keep everybody separate.

Mac was checking out a house in Sherwood Forest Estates, when his cell phone vibrated on his hip... It was a text from ET:

"LOS JUST PULLED UP."

Mac wrote the number of the housing company onto a napkin, then pulled away from the curb. Sherwood Forest estates, it was home to a lot of old mob figures back in the 1940's. The sprawling mini mansions were well groomed, the neighborhood was quiet and affluent, with towering oak trees throughout the courts. Mac could see living there within the near future.

ET and Los were sitting out on the porch, laughing and drinking, when Mac pulled up in the Maserati. Mac could see the smile freeze on Los' face when he saw that it was him behind the wheel.

"Surprise!" Said ET, slapping Los's arm.

Mac got out at the curb and quickly crossed the front lawn. Los was slow to stand.... he was too busy appraising Mac from head to toe.

"What up doe?" Asked Mac, pulling Los in for a hug.

"Ain't shit. Damn, my nigga, when you get out?" asked Los.

Mac took a step back smiling. "Shit... I been home over a month now. About a month, right ET?" asked Mac.

"Yeah, about a month," agreed ET.

Why y'all ain't hit me up?" asked Los.

"Bruh said you was on the road doin' ya' thug thizzle. Shit, I figured we'd get up sooner or later." said Mac.

"I see you ain't waste no time getting' to the bag. What chu' got goin' on?" asked Los.

"We gon' rap." said Mac.

Los had picked up some weight and his hair line was

thinning, but other than that he still looked the same, with his baby face.

"What cha'll niggas wanna' do? Let's hit the club." said ET.

"This nigga always wanna' hit the club." laughed Mac.

"Like I don't know," laughed Los.

"Come on, I heard they got some new hoes up at All Star's." said ET.

"Shit, it's on y'all." said Mac.

"Let's ride." said Los. "I wanna' see how this pretty ma'fucka ride anyway." said Los, walking toward the Maserati.

"Catch," said Mac, tossing Los the keys.

ET shot Mac a side-eye.... Mac hadn't even let ET get behind the wheel of the Maserati yet, and he was with him every day.

Los was like a kid in a candy store, as Mac showed him how to let the top down. Mac sat in the passenger seat while ET rode in the back with his mug twisted.

The radio dial was set on 98.7 Jams.... "I'm a Chedda Boy" by the Eastside Chedda Boyz came on, and Los cranked up the volume.

"Oh shit, remember this?" Asked Los.

Los and Mac nodded to the beat and rapped the lyrics of Jesse James, as they flew down Linwood. It was like old times again.

When they made it to All Stars up on 8 Mile Rd the parking

lot was semi filled with foreign cars being valet parked. Dancers on their way in to work lugged suitcases on wheels across the parking lot.

They valeted the whip and Los paid the door fee.

"Everything's on me tonight, my nigga. It's the least I can do," Los told Mac, as they entered the club.

Mac gave Los some dap. "It's all good."

A sexy yellow bone chick dressed in a tiny waitress outfit approached them by the stage.

"What can I set y'all up with tonight?" she asked.

Los took the lead, eyeing her thick frame from head to toe. "We good right here. But uh, send us some bottles of Spade... and uh, come check on me in about a half-hour."

The waitress smiled and turned towards the bar. Her plush yellow ass cheeks bouncing with each stride toward the bar.

They took up a table around the stage, where two thick brown skin chicks performed on the poles. The bar stools were occupied by hustlers and the booths were also being occupied.

The DJ was spinning a mix from the early Cash Money Days.

Mac tapped ET's arm, gaining his attention.

"You a'ight, my nigga? You ain't said shit since we left the crib." said Mac.

"Yeah, I'm straight," lied ET.

The waitress came back with three bottles of Ace of Spade. Los paid for the bottles and gave her a hefty tip.

"Here, and bring us some singles." said Los, giving the waitress another $3,000.

A sexy, petite dark skin chick crawled into ET's lap and started kissing at his neck. She was stark naked.

"Hey, daddy. I've missed you." said the female.

Mac and Los elbowed each other, laughing at ET.

"That's why this nigga wanted to come here." said Los.

"This niggas a regular," laughed Mac.

ET mouthed the words "Fuck y'all." as he stood up with the dancer. She led him by hand behind the black curtains of VIP.

"ET wonder why a nigga don't never put nothin' in his hand.... As soon as he get some paper, he up in one of these spots trickin' it all off." said Los.

Mac had to wonder if what Los was telling him was the real reason why ET said that Los wasn't the same. Los seemed to be the same to Mac, and what he'd said about ET seemed to be dead on, as far as him always tricking.

The waitress came back with their singles.

"Save some for me now," she flirted, as she sat the tray of money down and sashayed off.

Los handed Mac what he assumed to be half of the money

and they started tossing dollar bills onto the stage, as the two naked dancers went in, performing a simulation of sexual acts on each other.

"I'm glad you're home, Mac."

"Me too," smiled Mac.

"You know, it ain't too late for us to touch the kind of paper we were suppose to see before you got locked up."

Mac thought about their time together.... and their time apart. He wasn't denying that they were supposed to get rich together, that was always the plan. Life had just taken them in different directions.

"You seem to already have a head start. We come together and shit'll be a wrap." suggested Los.

"What chu' got in mind?" asked Mac.

Los flashed a wide shit grin, then patted Mac's shoulder. "We'll chop it up tomorrow. Tonight, let's celebrate you being free and us back together as fam."

Los raised his bottle for a toast, and Mac touched his bottle against Los'.

They balled out until the club closed. Los and Mac took two bad yellow strippers to the room, while ET dipped off with the girl who had him up in VIP all night.

Chapter Twenty-Five

Los hadn't changed a single bit in Mac's eyes, he was still a big kid at heart, always laughing and joking. Los woke Mac up, putting his finger to his lips.... Because he didn't want to wake the stripper's asleep beside him in bed.

Los was fully dressed, and he urged Mac to get dressed and come on. They snuck out of the room, leaving both strippers asleep and without a ride.

"Fuck them hoes." said Los, as they stepped onto the elevator of the Double Tree.

"You foul ass fuck bruh," laughed Mac.

"Shit... Foul would be taking that five hunid' back we gave they thirsty ass."

Mac couldn't do nothing except laugh, only because he knew Los wasn't joking, and he was surprised he hadn't clipped them for the money.

The elevator touched the ground floor and the doors

opened. "Let's get some breakfast," said Los.

"Yeah, and you can finish telling me about this million dollar plan." said Mac.

They ate at the IHOP off Jefferson Ave. The place was packed with ballers and sack chasers who'd been partying all night, and needed to settle their stomachs with some hot food and grease.

Mac and Los took up a small booth facing the flowing morning traffic on Jefferson Ave. They both ordered the Western Omelet and blueberry pancakes, just like old times after grinding all weekend on The Porch.... they'd hit up IHOP and pig out.

"So, what's up?" asked Mac, in between bites.

"I know ET told you, I stay on the road."

Mac nodded. "I'm listening."

"That's where the real flip is at, my nigga, going outta' town. Niggas for example in Cincinnati payin' every bit of twenty-eight, some thirty for a block. And that's all through Ohio."

Mac took a sip of his orange juice...

"So, where I come in at?" asked Mac.

"Shit.... whatever you send me outta' town wit', we split the profits. I got niggas right now ready to spend whatever, they just too scared to send they money outta' town, so they'd rather wait until the shit hit the street, and they'll pay the extra tax. Which is where I come in."

A beat passed without Mac saying anything.... He hadn't told Los, he was moving bricks and Mac was certain ET hadn't told him either, because of the way ET was speaking bad on Los being out for self.

"Los, how you know I got the type of work you're talkin' about in the first place?"

"What's understood don't need to be explained, my nigga. Since you been home I know you either left the pen with a plug or Ebony put you on."

Mac couldn't front on his nigga. Los was family and on top of that, the nigga had always been a hustler.

"When was the last time you spoke to Ebony?" asked Mac.

Los sighed and looked away. "Sis, ain't fuckin wit' me right now. She mad over a deal with this nigga she put me onto, but I don't wanna' talk about that weak ass shit. What we gon' do? You fuckin' wit' ya' manz, or not?"

"Yeah, we gon' do somethin'," The words came out before Mac realized he had just agreed to whatever Los' plan was.

Mac told himself, that he could never deny Los, on any level. Even though Los hadn't been there while Mac was in the Pen, Mac chalked it up to survival.... Los was out there trying to survive and duck the Pen just like every other nigga in the game. That didn't stop them from being family.

Chapter Twenty-Six

Los was in a rush to get back to Cincinnati, he claimed that he had a few niggas waiting on him to get back with some work, so they could get on. Los told Mac that these niggas would just about buy anything, but if they were to run across some A-1 they'd be all in only copping from them.

"Look, my nigga. I'm not finna' go outta' town," Said Mac. He and Los were cruising down Joy Rd with the top down on the Maserati.

"And you don't have to, I'm a make the run."

"So, what you talkin' about takin'?"

"At least five bricks."

Mac sighed at this. Five bricks was a lot to be sending out of town right now. Anything could happen, and he'd be stuck with the lost. And the last thing Mac wanted was to come up short with Solomon, especially on their first time doing business.

"I tell you what, my nigga. You say that you got some niggas waitin on you, right?"

"Facts."

"That mean you should have some dinero then, right?" Mac looked over at Los. "Money," said Mac.

"Yeah... I got about forty bands with me."

Mac nodded, while deducting the $40,000 from the five bricks Los wanted evidently on consignment.

"Gimmie the forty though, and I got chu'." said Mac. He reluctantly agreed to front Los the work, really going against his better judgment. Not that he didn't trust Los. But the game wasn't about trust, it was about winning. And in order to win Mac knew he couldn't start off losing.

Los was all smiles, as he told Mac to drop him off at ET's crib, so that he could retrieve the $40,000 from his rental.

They made the rest of the drive in silence, allowing the radio to fill the void. Mac felt as if Los had come on strong and was forcing himself on him.

When they made it to ET's crib, Los dug out the bread from the trunk of his rental car and gave it to Mac.

"See you in a minute," said Mac.

ET was out on the porch with his shirt off, and barefoot rubbing his stomach. He had a sly grin on his face, as Los climbed the stoop to the porch.

"Where bruh goin'?" asked ET.

"He about to grab some 'em real quick."

They both watched as Mac turned off Linwood.

"Los, don't' get bruh in no shit."

"Nigga, what the fuck is you talkin' about?"

"Just what I said." warned ET.

ET didn't know the details of what Los and Mac had going on, but whatever it was, ET was sure Mac would come out on the losing end when the smoke cleared. ET didn't know why Los had changed the way he had, but truth be told, Los was out for self on some cut throat shit, nobody was exempt.

Los sat in his car waiting on Mac to pull up, so he could get back in traffic. Los wasn't trying to hear what ET was rapping about, that's why he stayed broke, and waiting on somebody to do something for him. Not Los, he had always been the type to make it happen. His heart had grown cold over the years for many reasons, but the main one was the fact that he was never reunited with his siblings after years of bouncing around the foster care system. He told himself, that it's a cold world, so he's got to be cold-hearted in a world that doesn't love him. Los would do anything to get over if he could.

When Mac pulled back up Los hit his horn to let him know he was in his car. Mac saw ET sitting on the porch with a fifth of

Remy on his lap, his face semi screwed.

Mac parked and retrieved the 5 bricks from the stash spot inside the van. He quickly got out with the duffle bag clutched at his side and got in the car with Los.

Mac tossed the bag on Los's lap and checked his side view mirror for the law.

"Dawg, that's five of 'em. When I'm a see you?" asked Mac.

"Give me a few days and I'm a shoot back to the crib." said Los. He was smiling, as he inspected the bag.

They met eyes, with Los still smiling, and something clicked in Mac's intuition... Los gave Mac dap.

"Good-lookin', family." said Los.

His hand shake didn't match his smile... but Mac held his tongue, figuring he'd give Los the benefit of the doubt by trusting him on the work.

"I'm gone, dawg." said Mac, reaching for the door handle. He got out and Los cranked the engine. ET had his mug on as Los did a U-turn and drove away, honking his horn. Mac threw his hand up, as he walked up to the porch with ET.

"What up doe, my nigga? Why you lookin' crazy?" asked Mac.

ET hit his bottle of Remy, eyes glued to Los tail lights... "I hope you ain't gave bruh nothin' you can't afford to lose."

Mac's eyes were watching Los fade against traffic.

"What's up with you and Los?"

"It ain't me, bruh. I keep tellin' you the nigga done changed. He been pullin' stunts, runnin' off wit' niggas work an shit. Why you think he ain't wanna'see Ebony?"

Mac waited for ET to finish.

" Because she plugged him in with some old nigga, and Los ran off wit' da man shit. I'm tellin' you bruh. We gon' have to bury Los."

"I ain't finna' kill bruh." said Mac.

"We ain't, but what we can't do is stop the streets from killin' 'em."

Mac sighed at this realization. If Los was out there as bad as ET portrayed, then it was only a matter of time before somebody took him out.

"I'm a sit 'em down and talk to 'em. See where his mind at." said Mac.

"He on some fuck the world shit." said ET, then took a long drink from the bottle.

Chapter Twenty-Seven
One Week Later

Mac opened up five crack spots on the east side, selling double-up's and using neighborhood young hustlers as partners in each spot. He eventually made a few contacts up at Al's Barber Shop, where he was able to establish a relationship with some major player's buying 10 bricks at a time, all cash and no shorts. And the young nigga, Dae Dae was doing good, running through 2 bricks a day. Mac saw promise in him, so as long as he stayed loyal and stacked his paper.

Everybody on his team was on their A game, ET was doing numbers in Linwood, and talking about opening up another spot further west. But no word or sign from Los. Mac wasn't the type to be blowing no niggas phone up about no money. He only tried Los' cell once, and that was out of concern.

'Maybe he got jammed up or some 'em', reasoned Mac.

He and ET were cruising through the city with the top down

on ET's brand new cranberry Viper.

"Bruh, I know you wanna' believe anything, except the truth. But the truth is, Los done ran off."

Mac was looking out of his window at the passing souls along Gratiot Ave.

"What chu' give him anyway?" asked ET.

"Nothin' major, feel me?"

Mac couldn't help but feel played. He had real love for Los and ET. They were his brothers, and it was always understood that they'd get rich together, and die together if it ever came to that.

Where you at my nigga? Thought Mac.

Meanwhile, Los was in Cincinnati, Ohio with no intentions on going back to Detroit any time soon. He had come up on 5 whole bricks for $40,000. He whipped one brick into two and paid the niggas who sent him to Detroit to cop with that.

Los was on top of the world, selling nothing but 8 balls to the hustler's and fifties to the fiends. He had put together a little team since he'd been going out to Cincinnati. Skrow and Nutt were his two young hustlers on the rise. Los saw the hunger in Skrow and Nutt eyes early on, they had a trap on Back Street, pumping dimes and twenties. What Los liked the most about Skrow and Nutt, was that they always flipped their money. Every time they came to re-up, it was always double whatever their last order was. Los was loving them even more because they was slow to the whip game, and they were buying hard, gram for gram, with no complaints.

Los had a spot on Vine Street that he used to cook-up and conduct business. The apartment really belonged to Martina, a little slut he met years ago, when he first started making trips to Cincinnati. Martina had two little kids, a boy and a girl. All she wanted was something on her rent, some dick, and a few dollars. In exchange, Los had her house for whatever he needed it for. He stashed work there, guns, and made plays from her two-bedroom apartment.

"Bae, I need some money for my hair an nails," said Martina, standing over Los at the glass dining room table.

Los was seated with a burning blunt at the corner of his mouth, and a fist full of bills in hand, counting the days profits. Money lined the table in piles by denominations.

"You hear me, Bae?" Asked Martina, in her sexy voice. She rubbed Los's neck, then straddled his lap, so that their eyes were face to face.

"Tina, don't chu' see me countin' this money?" asked Los.

Martina was a short and thick red bone, with long weave, pretty face and flat stomach.

She grinded her pussy against Los's crotch, smiling devilishly.... "All this money is makin' me wet, Bae." she whispered into his ear, then ran her tongue around his earlobe.

Los could feel the heat of her phat pussy.... the only barrier being the short shorts she wore.

"What we gon' do about my pussy being so wet, Bae?" asked Martina, now biting her bottom lip, and looking Los in the eyes.

Just as Los palmed her soft phat ass there was a knock at the front door.

"Yo, Los. It's Skrow and Nutt!"

"Bae, get the door." said Los.

Martina smacked her lips, then sucked her teeth, as she got off Los's lap and headed for the door.

There was another quick knock, and Martina snapped. "Damn, I'm comin'! Shit!"

She unlocked the door and snatched it open. A chrome 357 came crashing down over the bridge of her nose, sending her down to the floor. Skrow was the gun men. He stepped over Martina and rushed toward Los, who was reaching for his Mack-11 on the floor.

Two shots roared from Skrow's cannon, the second slug struck Los in the shoulder and spun him out of his chair.

Nutt closed the door, and yanked Martina to her feet, with his Glock pressed to the side of her head. Blood poured from her broken nose.

Skrow stood over Los with the 357 pointed down at his face. "Nigga, where that shit at?"

Los was favoring his shoulder, blood seeping through his fingers. "Dawg, that's all I got, what's on the table."

Skrow tilted his head to the side, then shot Los in the leg.

"Wrong answer." said Skrow.

Los cried out in pain. "Aghh!!!"

"Keep playin' and I'm a box yo' dumb ass." said Skrow.

"Bring that bitch in here," Skrow said to Nutt.

Nutt manhandled Martina over to where Los laid bleeding out.

"Bitch, I'm a ask you one time, where that shit at? Play wit' me, and I'm a kill both of y'all asses." said Skrow.

Martina looked down at Los... then she closed her eyes, thinking about her kids.

"It's in the freezer." said Martina.

Skrow gave Nutt the nod to go check it out. A few moments later, Nutt emerged from the kitchen carrying two kilo's.

"That's everything?" asked Skrow.

"Yeah." answered Nutt.

"A'ight, rake all that money up." said Skrow.

Nutt was carrying a book bag. He stuffed the 2 keys inside the bag, then cleared the table in two arm sweeps.

Nutt was a stocky brown skin nigga with with long dreadlocks, and a mouth full of gold teeth. Skrow was a short, fat, black ass nigga with shoulder length dreadlocks. They were hustlers, but jack boys by heart. They would finesse plugs until they saw the prime opportunity to rob them for a major lick. Los was their latest vic. They'd been baking him a cake for months, and today was the payoff.

Los had the white mouth, as he stared up into the barrel of Skrow's 357.

"Dawg, y'all got the shit. Don't kill us," pleaded Los.

Without mercy or any hesitation, Skrow pulled the trigger twice. Two head shots opened up Los's head like a fruit bowl. Blood and brain matter splattered the floor and furniture.

Nutt shoved Martina down to the floor beside Los.

"God, no!" screamed Martina.

Nutt stood over the whore, then gave her two head shots.

Chapter Twenty-Eight

Mac hadn't heard from Los in two weeks since he went back to Cincinnati. The 3 bricks he fronted Los set his profits back some, but he didn't let that keep him from paying Solomon his money. Mac went to see Solomon and copped another 50 bricks.

The main thing for Mac, was he had established his clientele, so from then on he planned to grow with every flip. He had his sights set on buying a home and to stack as many millions the game would allow him to within the next year. Then he would re-evaluate his position.

Ebony was still trying to bounce back from her break-up with Kevin. She had started a party promotion company, using all her contacts as her initial clientele. She saw it as a win-win situation because she loved to party, and so did so many others she knew who always paid to have a good time.

Ebony's first party was to be an album release party for a local rap group. Of course she invited Mac and ET. The party was tonight at The Network night club. Mac and ET said they'd show up and support the party. It would give Mac and Ebony a chance to catch up. They hadn't seen much of each other in the past couple of weeks, and Mac wanted to assure Ebony, that he was there for her as much as she'd been there for him.

Ebony was at her place getting dressed for the party, when her cell phone vibrated against the bathroom sink. She picked it up and frowned at the incoming call. It was an out of state number. She reluctantly answered the call.

"Hello?" she asked, with a hint of attitude.

"Yes. This is she." said Ebony. She listened intently and her heart began to race. "Oh, my God. Where?"

"I will... And thank you so much for calling."

She sat the phone down on the sink, and stared at herself through the mirror.... tears began to well up in her soft brown eyes.

"I'm sorry... I... I thought we had time to fix it." She burst into tears, crumbling to the floor.

Chapter Twenty-Nine

When Ebony didn't show up to her own event, Mac got worried about her. It wasn't like Ebony to stand up a city full of people who in one way or another made her world go around.

Mac checked his diamond crusted Cartier watch, Ebony was over two hours late. The party was a success, people were dancing and politicking. The DJ was spinning new records from the Chedda Boys, Mac was feeling the vibe, but he couldn't stop worrying about Ebony.

"She still ain't answering?" Asked ET.

ET and Mac had a VIP table decked out with bottles of Remy, Hennessy, and Moet.

"Naw, bruh." answered Mac, sitting his phone down.

"Somethin' ain't right," said Mac.

And before he knew it, he was on his feet with his car keys in hand. "I'm a go check on her, you post up in case she shows up."

"A'ight, bruh. I'm a hold it down," said ET.

When Mac pulled up to Ebony's crib her car was sitting in its normal spot, and all the lights were on in the house. Mac quickly parked and got out with his burner on his side. He let himself inside the house, and called out for Ebony.

"Aye, sis!"

Mac found Ebony curled up on the sofa with the TV watching her. Her eyes were open, yet they held a blankness to them. Mac tucked his gun into his pants and went to take a seat beside Ebony.

The first thing he thought about was Kevin putting his hands on Ebony again. Mac checked her face for bruises, but saw none. He stroked her hair....

"Eb', what's wrong? You got a club full of people asking about you. I'm worried about you, and you in here curled up crying, over what, that bitch ass nigga, Kevin?"

Ebony sniffled. "He's dead, Mac."

Mac wasn't sure how he should respond. He didn't have any love for Kevin. As far as he was concerned, it was fuck that nigga.

"You still loved that nigga, huh?"

Ebony looked at Mac like he was crazy.

"Of course I still loved Los'. If it were you, I'd still love you too."

"Wait... wait... Los? I thought you was talkin' about Kevin."

"No, Mac. They killed Los. The coroner's office in Ohio called me while I was getting ready, said he had me down as his emergency contact. Say that they've had his body for a week now. They want me to come identify his body."

Mac stood up slowly. He began to walk away slowly.

"Mac, say something."

"They gotta' be mistaken... I.... I just saw Los. We was just together. Naw, that can't be him."

"Mac, I know it's hard to believe. But Los' was out there, bruh."

"Why you and ET keep sayin', bruh was out here down bad?" snapped Mac.

"Because it's true.... I don't' know what got into Los after you went to prison, but he flipped the script on me and ET. On more than one occasion he showed me that he was out for himself, and didn't give a damn about who he hurt, as long as he got what he wanted."

"I was gon' sit 'em down when he got back and see what was on his mind.... Damn." said Mac, taking a seat beside Ebony. He put his hands over his face, flashing back to the last time he'd seen Los in front of ET's crib.

"I wish we could've made things right between us," said Ebony.

They sat in silence for a while.... Ebony began to rub Mac's back in comfort.

"We'll get through this." said Ebony.

Mac turned and looked at Ebony, both their eyes blood shot and stung with fought back tears. Mac wanted so bad to believe that she was right. He couldn't take any more pain in his life, and he doubted if she could either.

Mac caressed the side of Ebony's face with the back of his hand, catching a lone streaming tear, brushing it from her cheek. The eye contact was too much for Ebony to bear, so she turned her head away, but Mac returned her eyes to his. Then he pulled her close to his lips, pausing a moment, before he knew it their mouths were locked in a long passionate kiss.... Ebony closed her eyes and kissed him back...

"Mac cupped his hand behind her back and laid her down across the sofa, without breaking their kiss.

"Mac," whispered Ebony, as he explored her firm breasts.

"Ahh...." she gasps, as he found her swollen clit, parting her juices with greedy fingers. He plunged one finger inside her tight pussy, circling her clit with his thumb. Ebony found herself grinding into Mac's explorations.

Mac brought her to the brink of climax, then let up, leaving Ebony panting and fiending for more of his touch. She attacked his jeans, loosening his belt, then snatched out his manhood.... she massaged his growing erection from the base to the tip, while seductively looking into his eyes. When she had him rock hard and pulsating inside her hand, she began kissing down the shaft and back up to the head, engulfing half his dick in a passionate suck. She popped his dick out of her mouth, kissing and teasing the head until Mac couldn't take it any longer. He put his hand over her head and dug his fingers into her scalp, guiding her to the rhythm he needed....

But just as he let up, so did Ebony after she felt the first burst of pre-cum shoot against the roof of her mouth. She had a devilish smirk on her face as she straddled Mac's lap.

He lifted her shirt over her head, while she unbuttoned her pants. Mac freed her breasts from her bra, then hungrily sucked at them, drawing moans from Ebony. Her pussy was throbbing for Mac to be inside of her. She pulled away from Mac and stood up. He watched with pure lust in his eyes, as she stepped out of her pants, then bent at the waist to pull down her lavender lace panties. Mac kicked off his shoes, then hurriedly slid out of his pants and boxers. Ebony was on top of him in a flash, her wet and heated pussy grinding against the shaft of his dick. She helped Mac out of his shirt, then began kissing all over his chest. Mac palmed her soft ass cheeks, spreading them wide, until his shaft nestled between her cheeks. He couldn't take the foreplay a moment longer. He lifted Ebony by her waist, guiding her down onto the crown of his dick.

They both gasped and closed their eyes on contact. Mac tore into her tight walls... plunging balls deep, pausing a mere second, before plunging deep again....

Ebony was on the verge of being undone. Once Mac found his rhythm he began to slap Ebony's ass enticing her to find hers.... She moaned and dug her nails into his chest as she began fucking him back.

"Mac!" She cried out, looking deep into his eyes.

He slapped her ass hard and released her waist, allowing Ebony to fuck herself over. She arched her back into a C, with her head tilted back and she went for broke slamming her soft, plush ass up and down on Mac's 9 inch pipe....

"Aghhh! Fuck!" growled Mac, as he fought to hold back the brewing nut threatening to bust at any second. "Aghh! Fuck this dick," he commanded.

Ebony looked him in the eyes, while biting her bottom lip and fucking his brains out... It was a battle of the wills, who'd make the other cum first.

Mac was determined not to let Ebony win, so he flipped her over and buried her face in the sofa, ass up. He drove inside of her balls deep, drawing a soft moan and a screwed up fuck face, she moaned looking back at Mac.

Ebony reached back spreading her ass cheeks for deeper penetration, but Mac took this as he wasn't fucking her good enough, so he grabbed her arm tightly and used it to push and pull his strokes in and out of her throbbing pussy. This turned Ebony on because she liked being handled and fucked rough. She closed her eyes and let out a scream, as she shuttered and came all over Mac's dick. Her erotic moans and the softness of her plush ass was enough to send Mac over the edge. He gritted his teeth and sped up his strokes, then pulled out just as he started cumming... Ebony turned around and sat up, reaching for Mac's spitting rod. She took him whole in her mouth and jacked him soft, making him double over from the sensations....

She curled into his lap when they were finished. Her hand massaging the length of his dick.

"You gotta' give me a minute to re-up." smiled Mac.

"We've got all night." said Ebony, kissing his lips.

Their tongues mingled in a deep passionate kiss, and within moments Ebony felt Mac's erection increasing in her grasp.

"Round two." she whispered, with a sexy, sly grin, right before going down on him again. Mac laid back with his eyes closed.

Chapter Thirty

Mac woke up to Ebony shaking him.... He was in her bed drenched in a cold sweat.

"Mac, you're okay... you're fine." said Ebony, with her hand on Mac's sweaty chest.

Mac was wide-eyed as he sat up in bed...

"You're heart's racing a mile a minute," said Ebony.

Mac ran a hand over his face, feeling embarrassed that he'd had a nightmare in front of Ebony. He pulled the sheets off his legs, then swung his feet out of bed, giving his back to Ebony.

Ebony scooted close behind him, kissing his sweaty and chiseled back. "Mac, you know you can talk to me about it."

"Talkin' ain't gon' change nothin'." said Mac, in a low voice.

"It might. You never..."

"Leave it alone, Eb'." said Mac, standing up.

Ebony watched his naked backside disappear into her bathroom. She felt horrible for Mac. All these years later, and he was still being haunted by his mother's murder.

Mac turned on the shower and stepped inside. He stood under the warmth of the jet, allowing the water to cascade down his face and wash away the pain from his mind. He heard the shower door open, but didn't bother to turn around.

Ebony slipped in behind him and wrapped her arms around his waist, then leaned her head against his back. She just needed to be near him and assure Mac that he wasn't alone in his pain.

"I love you, Mac."

"I love you too."

Chapter Thirty-One

The drive back from Cincinnati was a long silent one.... Ebony drove her Benz, with Mac reclined in the passenger seat, and ET stretched across the back seat asleep.

They had been to the coroner's office, and without a doubt, they confirmed the body of Los. It was hard to accept for all of them, especially seeing the way Los went out. Nearly half of his head had been blown off. They'd have to hold a closed casket for Los. Ebony would make the arrangements for his body to be brought up to Detroit.

Ebony looked over at Mac.... he had a solemn expression, staring out at the open road ahead. She reached for his hand. He looked at her and mustered a weak smile.

"You a'ight?" asked Ebony.

Mac sighed and intertwined their fingers. "Naw," he answered, with a blow of breath.

Truth was, neither was Ebony. But she knew they had to

remain strong for one another. The only family she'd ever known was right there in the car with her. Ebony never talked much about how she ended up in foster care. She'd only shared her story with Los. That's what made Los so special to her, he understood her. And he was always able to put a smile on her face.

"What chu' smilin' about?" asked Mac.

"I was just thinkin' about Los, and the first time I met 'em. He knew he was a pretty boy," laughed Ebony. "And then you came along, y'all two pretty red niggas tellin' everybody y'all was brother's."

Mac smiled at the memories.... "We was," said Mac softly. *Always will be,* he thought.

Chapter Thirty-Two

After leaving the cemetery, Mac told Ebony and ET that he'd catch up with them later. They wanted to go out to eat, and just sit and talk about Los' memory and the old times. But Mac wasn't up to it. There was two things that he needed to handle.

He headed to see Solomon at his bar. Mac had the $750,000 he owed Solomon in his trunk. When Mac made it to Sheeba's, Ole' Solomon was behind the bar in his usual spot, listening to his numbers lady read off the hits from the night before.

Solomon broke back a wide smile at the sight of Mac crossing the floor. His eyes fell to the money bag at Mac's side. Solomon excused himself away from the heavy set woman perched on the bar stool.

"My man, Mac." said Solomon, waving Mac around the bar. "Always a pleasure. 'Sup, young blood?"

"Came to straighten my face." said Mac, as he followed Solomon inside his back office.

"You know your face always clean with me, shut the door." said Solomon, rounding his cluttered desk.

He situated himself in the leather chair, and watched as Mac poured out the money from his duffle bag onto the desk.

"That's everything I owe you."

Solomon didn't bother counting the money, instead he raked it into a bottom drawer.

"I think I've got another sixty right now, you can take those."

"I'm done." said Mac, firmly.

Solomon was caught off guard, and his smile turned stale. "What, you've found a better supplier on me? I think I've been more than fair, Mac."

"And you have," assured Mac.

"Then what's the problem?"

"No problem.... I think I'm a do something different with my life, that's all."

Solomon sat back and crossed his hands over his stomach. A genuine smile creased his mug.

"Well, good luck young blood. I hope everything works out for you, and hey, if not. You can always come see ole' Solomon."

Mac nodded. "Appreciate you, OG."

Mac turned and left Solomon sitting inside his office. He had walked away in good standings, and $1,500,000 to the good. It wasn't nearly what Mac would have liked to walk away with, but he had to remind himself of an old saying Burch El would always say regarding dreams and money out of sight. He'd say, *a bird in hand, beats two in the bush any day.*

Mac smiled to himself as he pulled away from Sheeba's.... In his case, he wasn't dead or back in prison. No, he was $1.5 million to the good and a world of opportunity in front of him.

Burying Los made Mac realize that the game would always be cold, and it didn't care who it took under. Mac's biggest fears were dying broke and in a lonely prison cell. But today he could put both those fears aside.

Chapter Thirty-Three

Mac was ready to start a new life, but there was that one thing from his past, haunting his life that would keep him from moving on. Greg.

All his life, Mac told himself that he'd find Greg one day and kill him for what he'd done to his mother.

And today was the day that Greg would have to pay for his sins. Mac had someone look him up under his government name, Gregory Donovan. Too much of Mac's surprise and anger, the bitch-nigga had turned his life around and was remarried with two small kids.

Greg had given his life to God and became an ordained minister. It angered Mac because to him, Greg had no rights to happiness. How could he be fortunate enough to enjoy a full life, when he single-handedly destroyed Mac's?

In a daze, Mac followed Greg from his suburban home to a plush park, where he played basketball with his two small mixed breed boys. Mac watched from his car, as Greg bounced the ball at the boys attempting to do lay-up's at the rim. Greg was full of life, smiling down at his sons.

Mac got out of his car and crossed the grass over to the court. He snatched the chrome .45 from his waist just as the boys broke out towards the opposite goal, one chasing the other attempting to score.

Greg turned towards the approaching Mac, and his smile faded at the realization of who Mac was, and the gun being raised to his head. Greg looked down the basketball court at his boys, then back at Mac. The boys hadn't caught what was going on.

"Listen, Mac.... that was a long time ago. I've.... I've changed." said Greg.

"Nigga, shut the fuck up wit' that weak ass shit. Get yo' ass down on the ground." ordered Mac.

Greg slowly raised his hands and bent down until his knees touch the cement. "Please, Mac. Don't kill me.... I've got a family to look after."

The boys stopped playing at the sight of Mac standing over their father, gun pressed to his forehead. Mac looked at the boys, then into the eyes of Greg.

"I'm sorry, Mac." Greg said, then closed his eyes and dropped his head.

Mac flashed back to Greg beating his poor mother over a piece of crack... Greg showed his mother no mercy, as he struck her over and over, beating the life out of her.

"Nigga, fuck you." Said Mac, then yanked back on the trigger.

Greg spun to the ground from the head shot, and his son's cried out. "Daddy!"

Mac stood over Greg and let the clip ride out in his chest and face.

Once his clip was empty, Mac jogged back to his car. He could hear Greg's boys crying over his body. Maybe they'd have nightmares for the rest of their lives, thought Mac as he peeled away from the scene. He was definitely feeling an adrenaline rush after killing the man that murdered his mother.

Epilogue

Ebony was in full support of Mac leaving the game for good. She was so happy, that she decided to throw him a party. Since he never had an official welcome home party, this one would make up for it and hopefully all the years he spent behind the wall.

Ebony did it big renting out Chene Park, making it an All-White Affair. She was looking sexy in a flowing summer dress that exposed her back. ET and Mac had hit up Broadway's and City Slicker's, both donned in white linen and gator sandals.

The event was packed with ballers from all over the city. Many were there on the strength of Ebony, that and the fact that there were beautiful women everywhere.

Mac and Ebony were dancing to Jay-Z and Mary J's 'can't Knock the Hustle'. Ebony was lip singing the chorus as usual, all the while smiling into Mac's eyes.

"Baby, one day you'll be a star," sang Ebony.

"This yo' favorite song, huh? I bet chu' told the DJ to play this," said Mac.

"It reminds me of you." said Ebony, putting her arms around Mac's neck.

They danced until the song was over, then Ebony walked Mac over to the rail overlooking the Detroit River. She slid under his arm, and he kissed the crown of her head. The day was beautiful. Boats moved along the river, and a couple walked along the river walk.

"Tell me somethin'," said Ebony.

"Anything," said Mac.

"Okay. What are you gonna' do now that you're out the game?"

Mac looked out across the water....

"I'm a do somethin' that I've never done before."

"Which is?"

"I'm a live my life."

Ebony stood on her tippy toes and stole a kiss.

"I like that."

THE END

Contact Author Shawn "Nutt " McDaniel Sr
At
NSG PUBLICATIONS LLC
PO BOX 31303
Cincinnati Ohio 45219

Email address: nsgpublications45219@gmail.com

Business line: (513)544-3921

Instagram: AuthorNuttMcDaniel45219

Facebook fan page: Author Nutt McDaniel Sr

You.tube Channel : NSG RANSOM Jr.

You.tube Channel: NSG PUBLICATIONS

Website : HOME |
https://www.nsgpublications452.wixsite.com/nsgpublications

Also Available on Amazon...

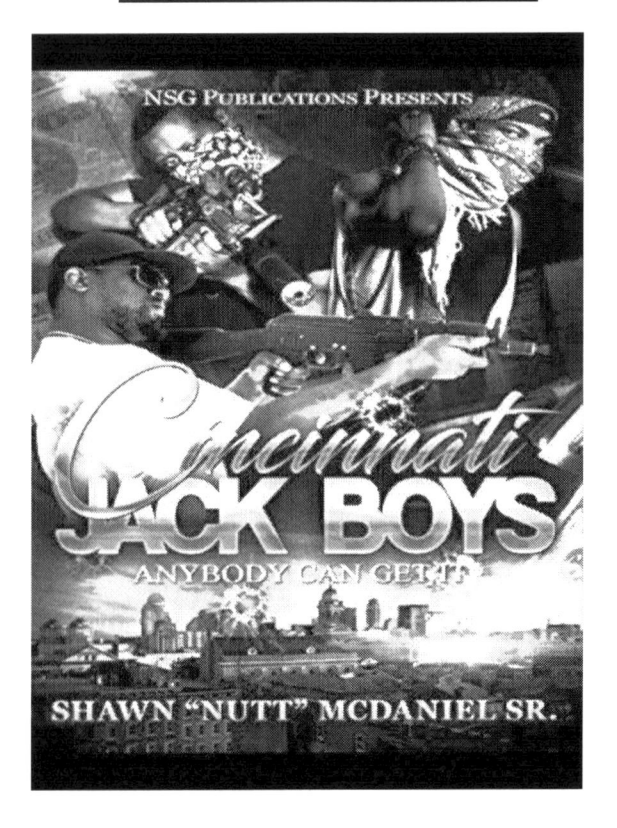

Cincinnati Jack Boys – Anybody Can Get It :
https://www.amazon.com/dp/B075CPVKHF

Coming Soon...

NSG Ransom - No Sleep Shit
https://youtu.be/guzC-X2zVKw

Follow the movement we got music, videos, books and movie clips coming soon. If your incarcerated look up this song. It's available on all platforms.

Support the Movement

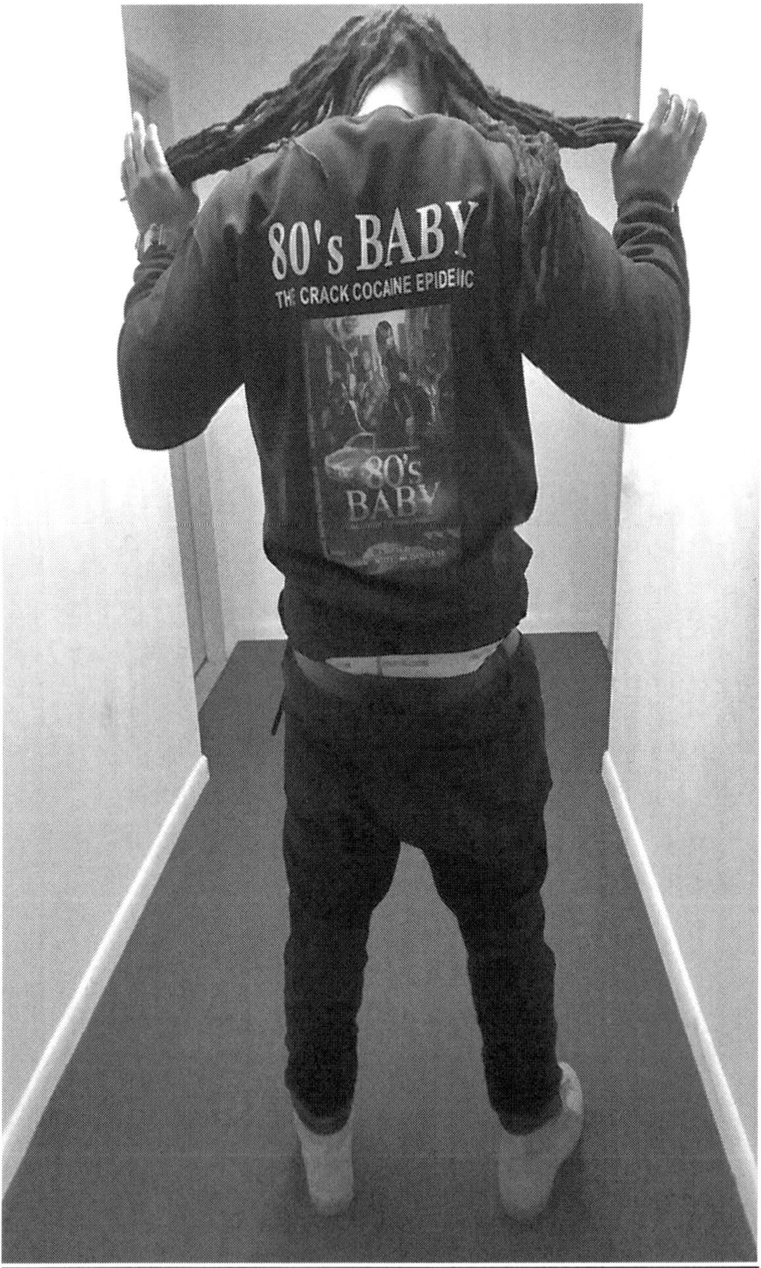
80's BABY
CRACK COCAINE
80's BABY

Made in the USA
Middletown, DE
19 July 2021